The
Will and Last Testament
of
Constance Cobble

The
Will and Last Testament
of
Constance Cobble

STANTON FORBES

PUBLISHED FOR THE CRIME CLUB BY

DOUBLEDAY & COMPANY, INC.

GARDEN CITY, NEW YORK

1980

All of the characters in this book
are fictitious, and any resemblance
to actual persons, living or dead,
is purely coincidental.

ISBN: 0-385-15800-9
Library of Congress Catalog Card Number 79-8499
Copyright © 1980 by Doubleday & Company, Inc.
All Rights Reserved
Printed in the United States of America
First Edition

To Bob and Mary-Etta
for their beautiful bodies
and to Gordie and Marion
for their beautiful house

The
Will and Last Testament
of
Constance Cobble

Under the staghorn coral, neon-colored fish hid in coral caves. Filtered sunlight became cool, liquid gray-green illumination, a private world with covert sea sounds and sea sights. An amethyst anemone waved to me; beyond, something else beckoned.

It looked like an octopus, an octopus of considerable size. I thought I could see its tentacles curling and uncurling in the depths. I treaded water, my flippers cumbersome, not designed for standing still. Octopi aren't considered dangerous, but I found all those suction-cupped arms unpleasant. Still, they're timid creatures, quick to scurry away.

Only, this one didn't.

I kicked with the flippers to move closer.

The tentacles weren't tentacles at all: hair, long, reddish-brown human hair coiled and uncoiled among the crevices of the coral reef. Small fish darted in then out in sudden dismay.

So did I.

On the surface, I spit out my mouthpiece, raised my mask and looked around for help. The others could be spotted only by the tips of their breathing tubes. I saw two snorkelers farther out and finally found the third ashore, on the sand spit behind me. I headed for land, it was closer.

A bit breathless, I flopped on the shore, removing my flippers. "Doria," I spoke over my shoulder, "there's a body down under the reef."

Doria Chase, bikini-clad and bronzed, squinted at me and asked, "What?"

I stood, pointed, and repeated, "There's a body down there."

Bright blue eyes widened. She shaded her eyes with her hand. "A body? A *dead* body?"

"I think so. Yes."

We stared at each other, then she said, "Anybody we know?"

"I think so."

Her lips formed the word *who;* no sound came with it.

"I can't be sure, but I think it's Pauline Gray." My mouth felt strange, not flesh any longer, but a leather flap that moved with straps.

"My God." Doria reached for her flippers. "We'd better get the men."

"Yes. And then?"

"Get her out."

"I'm not sure. The gendarmes, won't they want her left as she is?"

"But there might be something we can do—"

I shook my head.

She hesitated. "The gendarmes?"

"Well, yes. Pinel is French territory."

Doria frowned. "Not an accident?"

It was my turn to look wide-eyed. "An accident? Pauline Gray? No way, Doria. Somebody killed her."

St. Martin's gendarmes speak very little English, even though English is the common language on both sides of the island, Dutch and French. They speak little English because they are foreigners in the sense that they come from other French lands, France itself or perhaps Guiana, Guadeloupe, even Algeria. All four of us spoke some French, enough to exchange pleasantries, but the occasion required more than that. So, en route to the gendarmerie in Grand Case we picked up Antoine Beauchamps. Antoine, St. Martin-born, internationally educated, is an artist and a friend. He could translate.

We babbled at him as we drove. Greg was at the wheel, driving fast but carefully the way Greg always drove. My husband was relatively unflappable, thank God. Antoine expressed shock, smoothed his mustache with a hand colored blue and green. We'd called him from his work, he'd been painting acrylic sea-tones.

Sunday afternoons the gendarmerie is relatively deserted—one man on duty, the others at play, picnicking with families, fishing far out for shark and other big game. The gendarme on duty was young, fresh-faced, polite. Antoine explained.

The pleasant smile faded, the young face became serious. He produced forms to fill out, asked questions.

Vos noms?

Gregory James Brady.

Susan Foster Brady.

Allan Edward Chase.

Doria Henderson Chase.

The French made a big thing of maiden names for married women and middle names for men. Then they write them backwards without commas in between; thus Greg's name on an official communication always appears as Brady James Gregory.

Occupations?

Mr. and Mrs. Gregory James Brady, commerçants, shopkeepers to be precise, proprietors of a boutique in Grand Case.

Mr. and Mrs. Allan Edward Chase, owners and operators of a guest house in Marigot, innkeepers, on a small scale.

Born?

Almost the four corners of the U.S.A. are represented: Massachusetts, Wisconsin, Kansas, New Jersey.

When?

Pick a year in the thirties; the oldest of us, Greg, is forty-two years old.

Married when? The French are so thorough. Twenty years for Greg and me, sixteen years for Allan and Doria.

Now to the subject. Antoine again reported the discovery of a body, the location, the hows and wherefores. The young gendarme, making clucking sounds, wrote it all down. Then he called the main gendarmerie in Marigot and, hours later it seemed, reinforcements arrived.

"Do the women have to go back there?" Allan asked. "No need, is there?" Greg seconded Allan's suggestion.

Ah, *non. Les dames* could remain in the gendarmerie, this was business for *les hommes.* So Doria and I sat on the pier across from the gendarmerie and waited. We didn't talk much. I don't know what Doria was thinking but I was remembering the first time I'd met Pauline Gray. And the second, and the third. . . .

Cause and effect being the way they are, I suppose one doesn't open a diving school and operate a charter boat unless one looks good in a bathing suit. I mean, if you're built like a rum barrel, you tend to try and cover it up—this I've learned from our boutique business where we deal with all sizes and shapes from barrel to Pepsi Cola.

Pauline Gray, of course, looked great in a swimsuit.

She didn't look bad completely dressed either. For one thing, she had all that red-gold naturally wavy hair which she could wear coiled on top like a queen or pinned up here and there a la Brigitte Bardot in her palmy days or just hanging loose like some Medusa-Madonna. Madonna? Well, she had that kind of face. Fine bones and skin like golden satin. Plus green eyes that slanted up at the corners.

If I sound like sour grapes, I'm not—not really. I can appreciate a work of art even though I'm five feet two with a sawed-off thatch of brown-gray hair and a couple of pounds extra and out of place here and there.

Enough of that. I first saw her—*we* first saw Pauline shortly after we came to St. Martin to live. One of Greg's many unfulfilled ambitions was to learn scuba diving and so we went to Sea School, Greg to participate, I to spectate.

Sea School operated out of a cement block building that squatted beside Simpson Bay Lagoon. Anchored at a wooden dock were two thirty-foot boats marked with the stylized Sea School signature and further identified as Mermaid I and II. A small group of people had gathered alongside Mermaid II. Two of these were women. As we approached, one of the women, the taller of the two, raised her voice. "This must be our fourth student." She referred to a clipboard. "The late Mr. Brady?"

"That's right. Greg Brady. This is my wife, Susan. Sorry to be late." I opened my mouth, then shut it. According to my watch we were right on time.

"No problem." Pauline Gray smiled at him. "This is Phil Keith"—a young, rather sunburned man nodded a greeting—"and Allan and Doria Chase." The other woman and a big, well-built man said hello. The remaining three men were a part of the Sea School faculty: Pete, Dick, and Scott. They looked as though they lived in swim trunks.

"Okay." Pauline Gray wore a white one-piece swimsuit that meant business. "We're set, I guess."

She narrowed her eyes. "I take it you just came to watch, Mrs. Brady."

I nodded.

"Then, if you'll join me on deck I'll start my spiel."

We boarded Mermaid II. Pauline posed, her back to the wheel, her three assistants leaning against gunwales and the rest of us sitting at the feet of the mistress on cushioned lockers. Pasted on the glass partition above the wheel was a printed message: *Never dive alone.*

"The history of skin diving goes back to biblical times—even before. We owe an historical debt for influencing principles to such men as Archimedes, buoyancy; William Harvey, respiration; John Priestley, oxygen; Antoine Lavoisier, gas interchanged in lungs; and John Scott Haldane, nitrogen absorption."

I wondered how many times she'd done her spiel— she certainly seemed to have it down pat. She was a handsome creature, I thought—she rather reminded me of a wicked Esther Williams.

"But the true story of diving must lie with the inventive equipment and its development," she went on. "In days gone by divers used to be selected for their big feet." We all looked at our feet, and Greg grinned self-consciously. "Some diving historians give credit to a Frenchman, Captain de Corleu, for the invention of swim fins while others talk of American Owen Churchill's adaptation of devices worn by South Pacific natives. And some even cite Benjamin Franklin's autobiography which refers to a swimming 'sandal' that Franklin used.

"This same sort of controversy holds true for the

origin of equipment used for seeing under water. Ancient engravings show people employing a kind of face mask. Mass use of an underwater seeing device came through the travels of Japanese pearl divers in the late 1920s. Would-be divers set out to duplicate the bamboo goggles that the Japanese used and many fashioned face masks from large rubber hoses.

"The original snorkel was a reed tube of an escaping slave in the Nile Valley, or, if you prefer, the refinement of such a device for the German U-boats." She changed her stance slightly, creating a new picture of curves and angles. A breeze played with her hair, making a curl alongside one ear.

"The first self-contained diving dress providing a supply of compressed air seems to have been the work of an Englishman, W. H. James, in 1825. And in 1866 the Frenchman Rouquayrol developed a demand regulator for open-circuit scuba similar to that used today. The only thing was, the equipment was used with a surface connection because of the lack of a compressed air supply." She brushed the curl back behind her ear.

"Getting up to date, a French naval officer, LePrieur, developed a scuba with cylinders of compressed air with manual regulation of the flow of air and in 1943 Jacques Cousteau, then a French naval officer, put the Rouquayrol demand regulator on a high-pressure cylinder to produce the famous Aqua-Lung, the forerunner of similar devices used today." She smiled down at us. "End of history lesson for today. Let's talk about diving and you. Requirement one: physical fitness and by that I mean being fit for vigorous physical activity. Special note should be taken of ears (no permanent perforations of the eardrum, no predisposition to external ear infections), nose, throat and sinuses, respiratory system, circulatory system, eyes (a normal accommodation to light and distance), and teeth and mouth—don't laugh, malocclusions might prevent a solid grip on a mouthpiece.

"When you signed up you were asked if you suffered from asthma, ear infections, mastoids, chronic hay fever or sinus irritation, heart disease, or nervousness." She paused for another white-teeth-in-tan-face smile. "Most of you admitted to a slight case of nerves. We accept that—in fact, encourage it. It means you take diving seriously. But we watched you carefully for your reasoning ability because the greatest enemy a diver has is panic."

She clapped her hands suddenly. "Okay. A little action now. How about a quick swim, say out to that boat and back?" She indicated a catamaran moored some hundred feet away. "Just leave your gear here . . ." She looked at me. "I don't suppose you swim, Mrs. Brady, but if you do . . ."

"I swim," I said. "I'm just not interested in scuba diving."

She smiled. I wondered if her teeth were capped. "Well, then, it's getting warm sitting here." She gestured toward the water. "Be my guest."

With pleasure, I thought, peeling off my cover-up. I'll show you whether I can swim or not. Right from the start Pauline Gray rubbed me the wrong way.

I'd said that aloud now, not meaning to, and Doria

left off her study of an empty Heineken bottle rolling
at the surfside to tell me, "We needn't be hypocrites,
need we? I couldn't stand her."

"Why, I wonder? Nothing I can put my finger
on . . ."

"Me either."

"And yet, she rescued Allan."

Doria's head came up. "It infuriated him, you
know. He said afterward he was perfectly all right."

"Yes, he told us, too." Several times.

It had happened on the third day. Greg, Allan,
Doria and Phil Keith were thoroughly indoctrinated
(Boyle's law, thalassophobia, hyperventilation, equal-
izing pressure, currents and tides, the thermocline,
hydrobiology—moray eels bite like a bulldog if you
stick a hand in one's mouth; sea urchins look like pin
cushions and have brittle, sharp spines; barracudas
seem to attack only on provocation; the jellyfish's
tentacles sting like mad, ad infinitum) and this day
they would go down some sixty feet ("best diving
areas with marine life in abundance for prolonged
exploration range from zero to sixty-six feet"). Pauline stressed the time limit: "Sixty minutes is the
maximum but today we'll surface at forty-five minutes so synchronize watches, please." I watched them
disappear beneath the surface before I picked up my
book. *Don't Stop the Carnival* is recommended reading and rereading for island dwellers.

I'd just reached the cracked cistern crisis when
Greg and Doria reappeared. Moments later Phil
Keith, Pauline and her trio of helpers (I hadn't yet
figured out who was Pete, who was Dick, and which

was Scott) joined them on the surface. No Allan, but he was expected momentarily. I wondered if they'd whistled "America" on ascent; this was recommended for maintaining continuous exhalation in case of emergency such as loss of air supply. All very simple, but I had no desire to scuba-dive; the thought of real depths gave me something akin to claustrophobia. Thalassophobia was not my problem: I have no fear of the ocean so long as I know the surface is seconds away.

"Where's Allan?" I heard Doria ask Pauline somewhat anxiously.

"Just overstaying his time." Pauline sounded slightly irritated. "I'll go down and remind him that rules are rules."

One of her helpers offered to go, but Pauline refused the offer. We all waited for what seemed a long time, then the three instructors submerged as if on secret signal. Doria tried not to let a growing panic show. Just as her emotions were getting out of hand, Pauline surfaced; Allan was right behind.

"I'm perfectly okay," he sputtered later after Pauline had bawled him out, "I just lost track of time, that's all." But I noticed that he didn't protest in Pauline's hearing so maybe he had been in trouble after all.

"Here they come now." Doria, watching the road, indicated the gendarmes' jeep. The red French ambulance could be heard coming up from behind making that siren sound that European emergency vehicles make and reminding me of Nazi movies.

As we walked from the pier to the gendarmerie, the jeep stopped there, and the ambulance continued on its way. Greg, Allan and Antoine looked depressed, and the gendarmes' expressions were, as usual, inscrutable.

They had more questions, many more, but there was a recurring theme as translated by Antoine.

Who would have had reason to kill Pauline Gray?

One of her associates?

Pete?

Scott?

Dick?

Phil Keith?

Lila Debbs?

Cory Debbs?

Eloise or Mart Haven?

Who, indeed? Almost everyone who knew her disliked her.

But you couldn't tell the gendarmes that.

We had an unusual amount of local customers in the shop on Monday morning. Some of them came, ostensibly, to buy postcards or stationery or to pick up a paperback, but actually—and naturally—they all wanted the details on the death of Pauline Gray.

The island has what seems like an almost eerie method of prompt communication. Everybody hears about everything within minutes of the happening, or so it seems. A tragedy in Philipsburg or Marigot becomes instant common knowledge in Grand Case or French Quarter. Greg called it the sea grape vine and added, half-jokingly, that the message is carried on the trade winds.

Cecelia Trainer and Jessie Blair came through the front door as soon as it was open. They'd heard, they said, and wasn't it terrible? Had we really found her?

How and where and when? (We've learned to take the sea grape vine as at least half rumor until we've verified facts.)

I told them my part of the story and Greg took over from there. He looked tired, I thought; his blond hair, going silver so soon, was getting too long. He hadn't shaved immediately upon rising as he usually did. I had a hunch he hadn't slept well, but then neither had I. I kept seeing her swirling hair whenever I closed my eyes.

"How did she die?" Cecelia had prominent blue eyes, and they seemed even more hypertrophied this morning.

Greg told them. I looked at him, startled. He hadn't told me that.

"Really?" Cecelia's eyes bulged even more.

"How do you know?" Jessie tended to be forthright—some people said blunt. "Did you see the marks?"

"There was a chain, you could hardly see it till they got her out. It was imbedded in the flesh." He looked distressed at the sound of his words. "You know what I mean."

"A chain?" I asked. Up until now I'd clung to a faint hope that they'd announce it had been an accident. Sure, she'd been an expert swimmer and diver but accidents do happen.

Greg spoke directly to me. "Yes. Some women wear them with bikinis, around the waist. You said you didn't want to buy any for the shop, remember? You said you thought they were a silly fad."

"Yes, now I remember." A salesman had showed

me a sample, a thin gold-colored chain with a clasp
that let one end dangle at the navel. The ultimate in
slave-girl jewelry, I'd thought.

"Can you imagine?" Cecelia marveled.

"Well, I can tell you one woman who's probably as
happy as a goat on a golf green." Jessie enjoyed an island reputation for quaint speech. "Lila Debbs!"

"And what about Eloise Haven?" Cecelia smirked.

"Don't," I said before I could stop myself, "don't
say things like that. You could get them in all kinds
of trouble."

Cecelia bridled. "Well, everybody knows that
Mart Haven was just plain silly over Pauline Gray."

"And Cory Debbs made a damn fool of himself
last New Year's Eve." Jessie looked down her long
nose at the thought.

"But that doesn't mean they'd"—I stumbled over
the word murder—"do her bodily harm."

"Oh, doesn't it?" asked Jessie. "Lila has a wicked
temper, I happen to know."

"What have we here?" asked a male voice from
the doorway, "the Grand Case chapter of the St.
Martin Snide and Drum Corps?"

"Oh, Brett!" I turned, relieved. Not only was Brett
Carlisle handsome, charming, and a good friend, but
he had a wild sense of humor that could turn a
sourpuss into a sweet tabby within minutes. Every
woman on the island flirted with him and every man
liked him—he was that kind of guy.

I watched Cecelia and Jessie begin to purr; the
Carlisle magic never failed. Yet, we'd all been suspicious when he first came to live here. For one thing,

he was the world-renowned actor, director, husband
and then ex-husband to three of the world's most
glamorous and/or wealthy ladies. He'd be, we were
sure, filled with conceit, crude, probably a lush if not
worse, totally insufferable. But in the short time he'd
been among us, six months just about, he'd won us
over. Doria and I had even tried to play matchmaker
(Gillian Sparrow was a darling—rich, beautiful and
recently widowed) but Brett treated us all alike—
cavalierly in the best sense of the word.

"You've heard about poor Pauline Gray?" Cecelia
was saying.

Brett nodded. "Sorry you had to find her, Susan."

"It wasn't a pleasure," I admitted.

"What about the funeral?" he asked.

"We haven't heard," Greg told him.

"Where's her family?" asked Jessie.

"I really don't know. We didn't know her that
well," I answered. At almost the same moment, Greg
contradicted me. "She came from Cape Cod.
Hyannis, I think." He added, "She mentioned it
once. Said something about that's where she learned
to sail."

"Who would know?" Cecelia looked concerned.
"Suppose something happened to Ron and me—who
would know how to contact the children?" Her
plump shoulders moved in an exaggerated shudder.
"We should all make a list and leave it with our
maids—people to get in touch with in case of emer-
gencies!"

I heard a car brake, looked out to see who it was.
"Here's Gillian."

"Oh, Gillian"—Cecelia pushed past me—"have you heard?"

Gillian Sparrow, closing her car door, nodded. She looked marvelous, as usual. She had the figure for the halter-topped dress and her blond hair, worn long but coiled on top of her head, was perfectly arranged —also as usual. In a place where almost everyone sported a tan, her pink and white complexion was startling. She burned easily, she said, so she wore cover-ups and hats on the beach. Even now she reached inside the open window of her car and brought forth a big-brimmed straw hat. It was a nat- ural-colored straw, matching to perfection the beige linen of her dress and her bone sandals. I realized we were all watching Gillian, but Brett, who should have appreciated her beauty, seemed unaffected. I turned to look at him; his eyes met mine and he winked. I couldn't help grinning back.

The Greek chorus led by Cecelia and Jessie started up again. Everyone was searching his or her memory for any detail about Pauline that might lead to spec- ulation. I let them talk on, I had work to do. My seamstresses needed something to sew and I did the cutting. Men's shirts today, we were getting low on them.

Eventually they left, and a few tourists came in. Business was slow in this, the off-season, and Greg needed me to deal with the women who wanted to try on dresses. I wondered often what the gendarmes had found out about Pauline (and when and where she died and were there any clues as to the killer . . . wouldn't it be peculiar if they came to the conclu-

sion she hadn't been murdered at all, that somehow
that silly chain had gotten caught on something).
There were, however, long periods when I forgot her
completely and concentrated on our bread-and-but-
ter, the shop.

Antoine arrived on his motorcycle just before closing time. He thought we should do something about
a memorial service for Pauline and that surprised me
because I didn't think he knew her that well. I said
as much.

He wrinkled his high forehead. A young man, he
was already losing his fine dark hair. "I didn't know
her intimately"—his speech was as carefully considered as his etchings—"but she seems to be so all
alone. The gendarmes tell me they have been unable
to reach any family to date. We could have a memorial service. What do you think? Wouldn't it be a
kind gesture?"

He was a genuinely sweet man, I thought. "Yes, it
would, Antoine." Even if it made me feel a bit like a
hypocrite. "In a church? I don't think—I mean, did
she go to church?"

He shook his head. "I thought at the funeral home
in Philipsburg. Someone could speak a eulogy. If you
think not a minister, then I would be pleased to do
so. Unless you have someone more appropriate in
mind."

"I think you'd be fine," Greg told him. Antoine
served as a lay preacher now and again.

Antoine nodded. "I shall make the arrangements
then. Her co-workers have already spoken to me,
they want to pay any costs for the service. Will you

pass the word? The more who come, the better. Six
o'clock, perhaps? Do you think that would be suitable?"

Fine. Not only suitable, but convenient. The shop
would close at five, and that would give us plenty of
time to dress. Maybe we'd go out to dinner afterwards, the Rusty Pelican, where we wouldn't need
reservations, otherwise, Bilboquet. . . . I caught myself being what might be described as callous, but
she was not my friend.

It was hot, so hot on the day of Pauline's funeral. The men came in unaccustomed jackets, and even more unaccustomed ties.

The entire American colony had turned out, or so it seemed. Metal folding chairs stood in rows at the funeral home, all occupied by the time we got there, so we stood at the back and tried our best to look cool.

Hope and Hank Jacobs were there and Bob and Jane Schiller sat next to the Longmans. Behind them I saw Emmy and Kees Verschuur with Rush Little and George Steinfeld. I never knew that Pauline Gray was so popular. Even Lucy Sheldon was in attendance—she had been Pauline's competition (or Pauline had been her competition, whichever way it went).

"There's Chuck Dexter," Doria whispered. "I thought he was off-island."

There was Chuck Dexter, indeed, all two hundred-plus pounds standing six and a half feet tall, a figure hard to miss even in this unexpected crowd of mourners.

Chuck and Pauline had once been a pair a couple of years ago, but they'd split months back and he'd left his business, the local radio station, in the hands of Peter Richards, his St. Martin-born partner. We'd heard he'd been on Monserrat and then Tortola and finally St. Thomas, but here he was back—for Pauline's funeral? When had he come back? Did the gendarmes know about Chuck Dexter and Pauline Gray?

"There's a gendarme, see, standing there in the back in the dark suit." Doria was whispering again. "I recognize him, he was one of the ones who came from Marigot on Sunday."

A large floral spray stood at the foot of the casket and there was a blanket of red and white carnations lying across the top. "Who sent the flowers?" Doria wanted to know. I shook my head. Antoine, slim in a silky dark blue jacket and white pants, was coming forward. He looked, it seemed, at every face before beginning to speak. The only sound to be heard was the rustle of paper; two rows ahead Abby Giles was fanning her plump red face with some sort of pamphlet. I felt a trickle of perspiration run down my back. How could the men sit there in jackets?

"We have come to say farewell to Pauline Gray," Antoine began. "We have come to pray that the

Lord God in His wisdom has prepared a place for her in His kingdom . . ."

★ ★

"Hoo-hoo! Constance! Are you there?"

Constance Cobble, interrupted in the middle of Pauline Gray's funeral eulogy, silently took the name of the Lord in vain. One of her characters come to life, Agnes Goodwin (substitute the fictional name Abby Giles for literary purposes, heaven forbid one should be sued even though it was hardly likely here on St. Martin). . . . Damn the woman, here she came trotting across the gallery, couldn't she see Constance was working?

"Good morning, Agnes." Constance let her reading glasses drop the length of their chain, and sat back in resignation. She'd calculated a visit from Agnes was good for at least an hour; Agnes was deaf to polite hints while behavior verging on rudeness simply passed right over her curly red wig.

"Have you heard? You can't have heard, I just found out myself and you hide out here like a hermit, I don't know when I've been so upset." She collapsed in a wicker chair, literally bent her knees and dropped her two hundred (maybe more) pounds.

Constance winced for her old chair. Hard to get good wicker anymore. . . . "I suppose I haven't heard and I never will unless you tell me what you just found out."

Agnes leaned forward and the chair protested with a tiny creak. "Bootsie Baker has been drowned!" Her face grew even pinker in her excitement. "I think she was murdered." She threw herself back into the chair. "Now what do you think of that?"

Constance stared at her. It couldn't be a macabre joke—
Agnes was not known for a sense of humor. "Bootsie
Baker?" she asked stupidly.

"Yes, and how could she drown? An expert diver like
that? A party of picnickers found her off Anguilla, some
place named Shoal Bay. They say there's a lot of coral
there shaped like antlers, she was caught in the coral."

"Off Anguilla," said Constance dreamily, "not off Isle
de Pinel?"

Agnes frowned; she hated to be wrong but she often
was. It wasn't hard to spread false information on St.
Martin, where rumors ran rampant. "I'm sure they said
Anguilla. Shoal Bay. Is that on Anguilla?"

Constance nodded. "Stag's head coral," she murmured.

"What?"

"That's what they call the coral shaped like antlers.
Who found her?"

"I don't know. Some Anguillians, I suppose. Horace Albertson told me, but he didn't know all the facts—he got it
from the gendarmes and his French isn't all that good."

Horace Albertson, another character in the work in
progress but identified there by the name Chuck Dexter. I
should write a preface, Constance mused foolishly, like
the cast listing of a play—Agnes Goodwin played by Abby
Giles, Horace Albertson played by Chuck Dexter, Bootsie
Baker played by Pauline Gray. . . . What would Agnes
do if she told her that she, Constance Cobble, had just
drowned Bootsie Baker under another name?

"Murdered? Why do you think . . . she was murdered?
How? Strangled? With a golden chain?"

Agnes widened her guileless blue eyes. "I didn't hear
anything about her being strangled. With a chain? How

odd. I mean, I thought when a person was experienced in diving they know better than to wear jewelry. Doesn't it attract sharks? Didn't I read that someplace?"

Constance waved her to silence. "Yes. I mean, no. I mean, of course she wouldn't wear one in the water. I don't know why I said that. . . ." Agnes had a point there, but she couldn't know that Constance's plot accounted for the gold chain; why had she ever opened her mouth? A coincidence, that's all it was. Even the best of swimmers could drown. Bootsie had had an accident, that's what happened. Purely coincidental.

Agnes smirked. "Connie, I know you go into another world when you're working." She pushed herself out of the chair. "I wouldn't have bothered you, I really wouldn't have, except I thought you'd want to know, being a friend of Bootsie's."

Without meaning to, she said, "I wasn't a friend of Bootsie's."

Agnes wouldn't accept that. "Of course you were. She was always at your parties."

Not necessarily invited, though, but Constance didn't say that. Bootsie had a way of getting invited whether she was welcome or not. . . . Nasty thoughts to be thinking of someone dead. . . .

Constance caught her thoughts and brought them back to hear Agnes saying, "So as soon as I find out about the funeral I'll let you know, we can go together."

"I won't be going, Agnes. . . ." But Agnes was through the door and onto the gallery.

Just like Agnes. When you didn't want her, she came; when you wanted her to stay, she left.

She turned back to her manuscript. Antoine had been saying, ". . . a place for her in His kingdom . . ."

No use. No use at all, not now.

All she could think of was that Bootsie Baker had drowned and Constance felt as though she had done the drowning.

Tomorrow. Tomorrow she'd start again. Enough of the funeral, she'd start tomorrow right off with Morry Bunty.

★   ★

He was introduced to me as Morry Bunty and I thought, the man has eyes like a moray eel.

We were at a party at the Vernon Bells'. Somebody introduced us and then somebody shifted position and then I was standing next to this man with the eel eyes.

I said, "Hello, Mr. Bunty. Have you tried the caviar with sour cream?"

"Thanks. Live here, do you?"

I nodded. When I'd swallowed, I added, "My husband and I have a shop. You're a visitor, I gather. Is this your first time on St. Martin?" An easy guess; I'd never seen him before and he wore a suit and tie.

He, chewing now, nodded.

"I hope you're enjoying your vacation."

"I'm not on vacation."

What did that mean? Before I had a chance to ask,
Kathy Wilkinson appeared at my elbow. "Good evening, Susan. There's such a mob here that I haven't
had a chance to say hello."

"Hi, Kathy. Have you met . . ." But Morry Bunty
was gone.

"Who is it I'm supposed to have met?" Kathy,
bright-eyed, smiled up at me. Not that I'm tall, but
she's very petite.

"A man named Morry Bunty. He has—odd eyes." I
felt a little cold, there was something about the
Bunty man that chilled.

"Oh, him. Yes, Wilky told me he was here." She
leaned closer. "He's a detective from Miami."

"A detective?"

"Uh-huh. I think Brett Carlisle hired him to inves-
tigate Pauline Gray's murder. Either Brett or her
family. I understand she has a brother who lives in
Boston. A lawyer, I think. At any rate, Brett brought
Mr. Bunty to the party. Doesn't he have strange
eyes? Hooded and sort of yellow."

"Hello!" Brett Carlisle put an arm around each of
us. He had a drink in each hand; some of the drink in
the hand that held me dribbled onto my shoulder.
"Sorry!" He dropped his arms. "I'm not turning into
a two-fisted drinker, I'm taking one to Gillian." He
winked. "But I am just the least bit sloshed."

Gillian, looking like an inverted Easter lily in a
simple white dress with ruffled skirt, walked over to
us.

"Here, Gillian," he said, "is your drink. I was way-
laid by these charming ladies." Greg was beckoning

to me from the doorway. I murmured, "Excuse me," and went to see what he wanted.

"I'd like to go home, Susan." His eyes looked overly bright.

"All right. Do you feel okay?"

"I'm just tired. I've said our good-byes to Vernon and Joanne."

"Oh—shouldn't I . . . ?"

"No, not necessary. Would you drive? I'm just beat."

"Yes, of course." I was sure now he didn't feel well. We walked down the steps and out to the long drive; we'd parked way at the end. Candles in paper bags (to keep them from blowing out) lit the way. "You can take two aspirin before you go to bed. I don't want you getting sick."

He grunted in reply. Our shoes scrunched on the sand. "Did you meet that detective from the States?"

I glanced quickly, but couldn't see the expression on his face. "Yes."

"I wonder if the island authorities know what he's up to."

"What he's up to?"

"Poking around into everybody's business. You know he's here because of Pauline Gray?"

"Kathy said that's what she'd heard. But what can he do? He has no authority. Seems like a waste to me of her brother's money."

"Her brother?" We stopped, we'd reached our car.

"Yes. Kathy thought her brother, he's a lawyer, had sent Bunty."

"Her brother didn't hire him. Brett Carlisle

brought him over here. He's staying at his castle in
the clouds."

"Are you sure? Who told you?"

"The golden boy himself, that's who. Smiling all
the while through his capped teeth."

"Why, Greg—I thought you liked Brett."

"I can't stomach the son of a bitch. Come on, let's
go home."

Brett's castle in the clouds, as Greg called it, was
the most remarkable house on the island. It perched
high atop a rock-topped mountain (by geological
counts a hill, but on the island it seems a mountain).
The main building (front and center) housed a huge
living room (with fireplace), formal dining room,
fantastic kitchen and den that led onto a terrace. All
along the frontage set into the terraced side of the
hill was a swimming pool where one could see waves
when the wind was blowing. And the wind often
blew up there, thus the fireplace.

Running from the main house right and left were
catwalks that led around outcroppings of boulders to
bedroom suites. Those buildings were octagonal-
shaped, mostly glass. The catwalks had sturdy
railings because of the brisk winds. The illusion of a
castle was enforced by what appeared to be a battle-
mented building that housed three separate cisterns
to provide the estate with water. Brett hadn't built
and didn't own the house; he leased it.

The two houses directly below the castle belonged to the Debbs and the Havens. The house below them, at lower road level, had been occupied by Pauline Gray. Unlike the other homes in the area, this one was unattractive, mostly because it had never been finished. It looked as though some mad builder had been in charge of construction. When one unpainted cinder block building was cemented together, another separate one sprung up. The complex, if that was what it was meant to be, was strung together by a head-high fence of sorts made of decorative blocks, i.e., cinder blocks with holes that formed a pattern. The overall effect was that of a somewhat grim compound in progress, and this started the trouble between the Debbs and Havens, acting in double tandem, and Pauline Gray.

Lila and Cory Debbs had retired to St. Martin five years before when they were in their early sixties. They'd been married so long they'd begun to look like one another, or so Greg said. There *was* a resemblance, mostly one of expression, I thought, and the first impression I got from Lila and Cory was "there's a persnickety pair." Their house was their life, now that they had little else to do. Everything in it was just so, colors coordinated, furnishings scaled exactly, garden meticulously manicured. Pauline Gray's careless abode just below their perfect world constituted an irritation that gradually became an open sore.

Eloise and Mart owned a nice home too, although not as precise as the Debbs house. The appearance of the Gray residence annoyed them, but they bought and planted dozens of hibiscus which, prospering

under Eloise's green thumb, effectively screened the
Gray property from Haven sight. What they couldn't
screen out was sound. The prevailing winds blew in
their direction, rather than the Debbs's, so the
Havens got the full benefit of Pauline's stereo, radio
and tape recorder, Pauline's frequent and noisy
guests, and—worst of all, according to Mart—
Pauline's big police dog who barked, declared Eloise,
all day and all night.

All this we had heard in great detail from both
wives; the habits of Pauline Gray had become, in
fact, just about their sole topic of conversation. People began to avoid them—at least, we did. What
could you say when you'd heard the story for the
tenth time?

But, as I told Greg, people simply do not drown
somebody just because they're an annoying neighbor.
"It could have been some kind of freak accident," I
suggested.

"The gendarmes don't think so," he snapped. He'd
been very edgy of late. I wondered if he should see
Dr. Gibbs; maybe he was coming down with something.

"All right, so I was only wishing aloud. The whole
thing makes me feel—I don't know, like a cold cloudy
day. And that Bunty man gives me the creeps. Why
in the world do you suppose Brett is giving him
houseroom?"

"I think your friend Brett simply likes to meddle.
He's playing his god role."

My friend? Greg's friend, too, I'd thought. I collected some tactful words to pursue that subject fur-

ther but Greg got up to open the shop doors even though my watch told me it was ten minutes to nine and we didn't open until nine. Maybe my watch was slow or perhaps Greg didn't want to discuss Brett—or Pauline. I went to help open up, saw that the sky was its usual brilliant blue, but still I felt clouds, dull clouds, Gray clouds—yes. Gray clouds. Damn the woman! There was a snake in Eden.

✦   ✦

Constance was in the process of doing something she disliked; she was filling out a form for *Who's Who in American Women*. One reason for her distaste was the feeling that there was something slightly degrading about reporting on one's accomplishments; it smacked of boasting. Another reason was the publication itself. Why American women? There was no special listing for American men. And lastly it irked her just a little to be ignored by *Who's Who* sans designation and yet she knew that by literary standards she was strictly a lightweight. Nonetheless, she felt like throwing the whole thing into the wastebasket except that they might publish the listing exactly as they had previously and it was out of date.

She had, for instance, moved to St. Martin three years before, but they still had her stateside address. She'd had four books published that were unlisted. And, worst of all, it still listed her as the wife of Roger W. Cobble, who had been dead now for four years. That was, she thought, a terrible thing to do to Roger, ignore his passing. It was her fault, she'd admit that—she hadn't replied to previous requests for an updating of her listing. But now, sighing, the time had come.

Name — Constance Elizabeth (Fielding) Cobble, check.
Address — Post Office Box 1111, Marigot, St. Martin,
          French West Indies. Cross out old U.S.
          address.
Born — No change there. She'd be fifty this year.
          C'est la vie.

Where it said wife of Roger W. Cobble she exed out wife and carefully printed WIDOW. She considered that for a moment. Should she eliminate all mention of Roger? People would remember that she had shot him. Accidentally, of course, but they might not remember that.

Damn, Agnes again. She heard her making her way up the steps. "Good morning, Agnes. How was the funeral?"

"Very sad. She looked terrible. It really should have been a closed casket. Everybody was there." Agnes took a deep breath; her face was flushed from hurrying. "You should have come," she went on, heading for the wicker chair.

"But I really didn't know her very well." And I won't, she thought but did not say, be a hypocrite.

"I hardly think that matters. We should stick together, you know, all we Americans."

"Who was there?" she asked, not caring at all.

"Oh, everybody. Bob Halsey, Lucy Sheldon, everybody from Island Water World and Lucy's diving school, of

course. Noblesse oblige. And the boat people, the Borahs
and, let's see, Bob and Mary-Etta and Stuart Denike and
Bill and De Forbes and most of the lowlanders, including
Jeannette Rockefeller. Everybody."

"Did her brother get here? I understand she has a
brother." Spoken absentmindedly.

Agnes frowned. "Really? I didn't know that. There was
no one there who belonged to her, that's what made it
so sad. Horace paid for the funeral, I think. And the
burying."

"The burying?" Constance hadn't considered that.

"Yes. No doubt he'll be reimbursed when her estate is
settled. He arranged for a plot in that cemetery down by
the Great Bay Resort Hotel. Really very sad." She
blinked, remembering. "But if she had a brother . . . ?"

"I must have been mistaken." Of course. She was mix-
ing fact with fiction. It was Pauline Gray who had a
brother, not Bootsie Baker.

"And another thing that's sad." Agnes leaned forward.
"Well, maybe not sad but strange. There were police at
the funeral. From both the Dutch and French side. Isn't
that strange?"

Constance nodded. Very strange indeed. Especially
when Pauline had died by drowning near Anguilla. Books
didn't get acted out in real life, especially those that
hadn't been published, and hadn't, in fact, been seen by
anyone other than the writer. Perhaps she should give
up—this one was bad luck. And yet she'd put in so much
time on the plotting, it had been going well—until now.
Ridiculous. She'd been spending too much time by herself. She needed to get out, see people, get a new perspec-

tive. "How do you know the police were there? Were
they in uniform?"

"No, but I recognized them. That nice gendarme
André whatever-his-name-is and Inspector Montesanto. I
know him because of the time I thought my wallet was
stolen . . ."

"Maybe they were friends. Maybe they weren't there
on official business."

Agnes looked disappointed. "I suppose it's possible."
She pushed herself out of the wicker chair. "Well, I've got
to go to Marigot. I hear the Gourmet has a new shipment
of French cheeses. I just stopped in to see how you were."

"Wait." Constance spoke on impulse. "I'll go with you.
We can have lunch at the Bouccanier."

"Oh, that would be fun, but—have you been to L'Aven-
ture? I love that terrace overlooking the bay. And the
food's quite good."

"All right, if you prefer."

"And there's La Vie en Rose. Whatever you want to do."
Agnes beamed, she seemed really pleased. "It's so seldom
you have time lately."

And since Constance felt guilty, they went to L'Aven-
ture where they encountered Horace Albertson and a
friend, Ed Quinn, who was visiting from the States.
"Won't you girls join us for lunch? What will you have to
drink? A Bloody Mary for you, Connie? You, too, Agnes?
Okay, waiter, we'll be four instead of two. Ed, these are
two of the ladies who live on the island. I told you there
are quite a few expatriates. . . ."

Constance, hardly listening, sat in fascinated silence.
This man, this Ed Quinn, had eyes like a moray eel.

Or was she imagining again? Perhaps, because when

she was halfway through her drink she looked at him and all she saw was a rather nice-looking middle-aged man with a friendly face.

"I worked for Horace once," Ed Quinn told her. "A dog's age ago."

"Then you're in radio." His voice was good. "An announcer?"

He grinned. "Once upon a time. Now I'm a disc jockey in Boston. The late night bloomer variety."

"The kind accepting telephone calls?"

"Right. My fans are the night people."

Constance had once listened to that type of show. "Isn't it depressing?" She'd thought so, still she'd listened.

"Hell, yes." He grinned again. She thought she glimpsed the eel in his eyes, but it went away when Horace spoke. "Don't let him kid you—he's a bleeding heart. Gets all involved. I tell him he'll end up on a psychiatrist's couch. I had to pry you away to get you here, so knock it off. You're on vacation, Ed."

Another grin, but there was no need to answer since Agnes was talking—complaining about something. Constance shut her ears off and concentrated on the menu. Ambrosia—yoghurt and bananas and apricots and walnuts. She thought she'd be able to get back to work when she returned home. From this new perspective, she could see that she'd been drifting into a private grotto, airless, where strange creatures hid among the rocks. She'd been there before. Out now. Shut the door. Come into the almost world that was.

Agnes' car moved noisily away down the drive, out to the road. She needed a new muffler.

Constance, slightly sleepy, climbed the steps to her gallery. She was determined to return to Susan and Greg, Doria and Allan and the rest of them. The net was out, being pulled in, just a little at a time so that hardly anyone would notice. . . .

"Home at last," said the big gecko clinging to the wall near the doorway. "Where the heck have you been? I've been waiting for hours—half an hour anyway."

The lizard's voice, a soft falsetto, was familiar. "I'm sorry." She smiled at the gecko. "I went out to lunch. You could have come with me if you'd only spoken up sooner."

"That's the story of my life. Did I ever tell you about the time I was introduced to this great white hunter?"

The gecko blinked its tiny eyes at her, blowing out the orange sack at its throat, preening. "Found out later he was really big-time. An alligator procurer. Could have made it to the top right there if I'd only told him I'd work my tail off at alligator school."

Constance laughed. "Come on out, Jerry. I thought you were off-island. When did you get back?"

Jerry Tosca put his head around the doorjamb and blinked like the lizard. "Got back a few days ago. Can't make it in the big wide world out there." He kissed her on both cheeks. "I was just writing you a note." He had paper and pen in his hand. "Noticed a work in progress on your desk. Do you want me to take my gecko and go?"

"Of course not." She was feeling too euphoric to write anything. "Let's sit out here where it's shady and cool. What can I get you? Anyway, he's *my* gecko. I don't mind you putting words in his mouth, but no fair lizard-snatching."

"Nothing for me, thanks." He smiled his sweet smile. "I came to lead you astray. Come away with me to Anguilla, for the weekend. We'll stay at Ruth Goodnow's. Separate rooms to soothe your middle-aged conscience. Even dutch, if you insist."

"What would we do in Anguilla?" It was a narrow flat island off the north coast of St. Martin—where Bootsie Baker had drowned. For a moment, she'd forgotten.

"I'm thinking of building over there."

"On Anguilla?" He'd been living at the Moulton house down the road for nearly a year. "You don't love us anymore?"

"It's getting too crowded. Alfie says so."

"Alfie's antisocial."

"True. Will you come with me? I'd like your advice."

"All right. This weekend?"

"Friday morning? The plane leaves at seven-thirty. Too early for you?"

"No." She was usually up by six or by sunrise, whichever came first.

"I'll pick you up at quarter of seven."

"All right." He kissed her again on both cheeks and took his leave. His car wasn't there, she realized; he must have walked. A medium-sized, medium-aged man with a sweet ugly face. A celebrity—once.

Once it had been Edgar Bergen and Charlie McCarthy *and* Jerry Tosca and Alfie. Edgar Bergen ultimately had won the unannounced contest but Jerry had given him a long run for his money. Alfie wasn't as abrasive as Charlie, perhaps that was why. The public preferred aggression, she'd decided. Personally, she thought Jerry a superior ventriloquist. His lips didn't move. Or, if they did, hardly at all. But it was unimportant: nobody watched ventriloquists anymore.

So, she was going to Anguilla. Curiosity? Never mind, back to the book. Back to Brett Carlisle et al, Brett who had been fashioned out of bits and pieces of Jerry Tosca with a reverse twist.

★   ★

On Sundays we usually went with Doria and Allan to the beach. Doria brought the Bloody Marys and we brought the beer. We both brought food. Sunday by the sea, a habit. Sometimes by boat, sometimes by car, whatever pleased us.

The Sunday following Pauline's funeral we drove

to the beach at Oyster Pond. A few others were
there, down at the far end. St. Martin beach proce-
dure: you don't bother us, we don't bother you. We
found a place under some grape trees and set up our
creature comforts: chairs, coolers, towels, assorted
paraphernalia.

"What a week!" Doria put her head against her
chair back, removed her dark glasses and rubbed her
eyes. "We've had an impossible group at the guest
house. One sweet young thing has never used a gas
stove, and is terrified to light it. The man upstairs
was fool enough to take a bite out of a manchineel
apple, so we had to take him to Dr. Gibbs. And a
third couple started out by picking up a couple of
horrendous sunburns. No matter that you warn them,
they *will* fry in the sun."

"I'm going in the water," Greg announced, getting
out of his beach chair.

"I'm with you." Allan followed suit.

"Greg seems kind of depressed," Doria observed.

"I thought Allan was awfully quiet."

"Has that Bunty man been over to see you?"

"Yes. Just a casual visit, he said. He looked over
the shirts but didn't buy anything."

"He was nosing around the guest house. I didn't
see him, but Allan talked to him."

We watched the men for a moment. They were
standing waist deep in the water, conversing.

"What did he have to say?" I wondered.

"I'm not sure."

I gave her a quick look. "Allan didn't tell you?"

"He said Bunty was interested in a possible reservation for next season."

"You don't believe that?"

"I would, except for the fact that Allan acted kind of strange when he told me—answered me, actually. I had to ask him what Bunty wanted, he didn't volunteer."

I considered that. "Greg was that way, too. He was with Bunty in the men's shop so I don't really know what they said."

"Inspector Montesanto came to see us, too."

"Oh?"

"He was very pleasant. Said he was verifying the facts. He asked us to tell him about discovering the body, and Allan said we'd been all through that. Montesanto laughed and said his French wasn't all that good."

"That's probably true."

She nodded. "Just the same, it makes me feel— funny. Vaguely guilty of something."

I knew what she meant. None of the gendarmes had been in but they had been in evidence. Across the street at Chez Christophene. Down at the corner. A couple at a time, chatting, looking very normal. Except that we didn't see them around that often. They were few and had a lot of miles to cover. "We couldn't help it if we were in the right place at the wrong time!"

"I can't figure it." Doria was still watching our husbands, now treading water farther out. "It would be just plain stupid to kill her and turn around and find her."

"Maybe they think that was the plan. Because it would be stupid. Especially if she hadn't been found. She'd have disappeared. No one would ever know."

"Maybe not." She nibbled at her lower lip. "Somebody didn't want to go that day. I can't remember who."

I stiffened. "It wasn't Greg."

"I didn't say it was."

"Maybe it was Allan." I couldn't help myself.

"I don't think so." She turned the glasses on me. "Was it you?"

I took a deep breath. "I wanted to go to Tintamarre but I didn't really care. You wanted to go to Pinel and the guys wanted to go to Anguilla but the channel was too rough."

"Yes. I did want to go to Pinel." She stood up and stretched. "I think I'll get wet. Coming?"

I wasn't ready. "What about Chuck Dexter?"

"What about him?"

"Why didn't they keep him on the island? I hear he's gone again. How do they know he didn't do it? He was crazy about her, everybody knows that. And she threw him over, everybody knows that, too."

"Do they? I didn't. I mean, I knew they were a pair for a while, but I got the idea she was the smitten one."

"That's not the way I heard it. And he could have slipped back here—"

"A man that size? Susan, you're grasping at straws."

I blinked furiously. "He could have flown to Anguilla from Tortola, and met her there in her boat."

"Except that he was in Miami that weekend."

"In Miami? Who says?"

"A whole convention of radio people, that's who says. Montesanto told us Chuck was a panelist for a seminar on Caribbean broadcasting. That's why they let him go. There was no way he could have done it."

The tears came. "Oh, Doria, why do you want it to be Greg?"

She stared at me. "Susan, that's the most horrible thing I've ever heard you say. I refuse to honor it with an answer."

"But it's true," I whispered.

She ran into the sea, dove beneath a wave and emerged near the men. We'd been friends, good friends, for a considerable time. We valued their friendships, it would be sad indeed if we drifted apart. Why was Doria so suspicious of Greg? Because she *was* suspicious, no matter how she denied it. There were some twenty thousand regular residents of this island, almost any of whom . . . It was that Morry Bunty who was setting teeth on edge, causing me to quarrel with Doria. Why had Brett ever brought him here, if he had? I'd ask him point-blank. Next chance I got, I'd ask him.

The next chance I got was at a party at Bill and Olga Denler's. The place was packed, everybody was there except for—thank goodness—Morry Bunty.

"Brett." I tugged at his arm. "This time I've got a bone to pick."

"Susan, luv! How are you?" The Carlisle charm was one hundred proof, as always.

"That Bunty man," I blurted. "Why is he here?
Everybody says he's a detective and that you
brought him here. He's making people . . . nervous.
You didn't even like her that much, did you?"

He peered down at me. "Why, Susan, your glass is
empty. Let me fill it for you. Gin and tonic with lime,
right? Morry Bunty is an old friend of mine, that's
all. His wife divorced him and he took it hard so I
asked him down to unwind." He took the glass from
my unresisting hand. "You know how this place is
for rumors. Morry isn't the long arm of the law, never
has been. He was a studio cop out in Hollywood." He
grinned down at me. "Now don't you feel silly?"

His grin was infectious. "Yes," I said. "Silly."

He sobered. Standing there with a glass in each
hand, he asked, "Are you that worried about Greg?"

"Go on," I told him. "Get me that drink before I
die of thirst."

Yes, I was worried about Greg. On the day before
Pauline Gray was murdered we'd gone our separate
ways. I to Philipsburg for a haircut and some shopping, he to Marigot to find a man to build some racks
for the shop. I didn't see him again until nearly
sunset.

★　　★

Ruth Goodnow's place on Anguilla consisted of four attractive one-story buildings, all with high ceilings and lots of doors and windows welcoming the trade winds' passage. Cool and pleasant, there was the main building which housed a huge living room with bar (more or less open on three sides), a small dining room for once-in-a-while inclement weather, a dining patio, kitchen, storeroom and living quarters for Ruth. Two of the other low white buildings were halved into big bed and bath suites, and the fourth was one king-sized unit (Jerry called it the honeymoon cottage).

He had one half of a double unit, Constance the other. And, somewhat to her chagrin, they were not the only guests. She noticed beach towels and swim trunks drying on the railing of the second double unit. Jerry, seeming to read her mind, said, "Never mind, Connie. It will be

someone we don't know, and will never see again. Your
reputation will be unsullied."

"Oh, Jerry, you make me sound like such a prudish old
woman. I have no guilty conscience. I don't care who it
is."

But, as it turned out, it was someone they knew. It was
Horace Albertson and Ed Quinn was with him. Constance had the idea that Horace didn't look any more
pleased to see them than she was pleased to see Horace.
But at dinner he was his usual hale and hearty self so she
decided she'd imagined it.

"The Thyeses' and the Tarberts' houses are done and
the Clarks' house is underway." Jerry was explaining his
reason for being on the island. "Ruth here has some more
land." He smiled his shy smile at her. "I'm hoping I can
talk her into selling me a parcel."

Ruth Goodnow was an American who had been living
on Anguilla for several years. She was, Constance
thought, typical of the several self-sufficient women she
knew who were capable of living alone and running a
business: good-looking, blunt, practical-minded and a little strange. Constance mentally apologized for the last
adjective; all of us, she thought, all of us women living
alone in foreign places have to be a little strange, herself
included.

"I'll take you over for another look tomorrow," Ruth
promised Jerry. "But I'm not sure I want to sell." She
eyed Horace. "How did you make out today?"

Horace helped himself to more langouste, then
shrugged. "Musical chairs," he said. "See the governor,
see the local nabob, see the opposition headman, talk to
this one and that, and be patient."

What was Horace up to, Constance wondered? Evidently he wasn't going to say, because he changed the subject. What was she here for, anyway? She should be home dealing with Susan and Greg and the rest of them.

What did Jerry want of her, bringing her here? And even more important, what did she want of Jerry?

After dinner, Horace suggested a game of bridge. Constance bowed out, took cognac and sat out on the gallery, listening to the sound of the sea. The voices of the card players blurred and she found herself in silent conversation with Roger. She used to talk aloud to him; perhaps this was an improvement?

I retreated like a good little girl, Roger, but I'm not doing as well as I'd expected. There are dissatisfactions, longings, Roger, that won't go away. When I ran to you where you lay bleeding all I said was, oh, my darling, but what I meant was I'll make it up to you. Somehow, I'll make it up to you. But now I see—how do you make anything up to a dead man?

Sitting there, listening to the sea, she found that her glass was empty so she went inside and refilled it at the bar in the corner. "Partner," Horace was asking, "why didn't you play a heart in response to my signal?"

"'Cause I'm just a stupid little dummy." Jerry replied in Alfie's voice. Constance went back to the gallery.

Concentrate on the next chapter. It was all plotted, where the next body would be found, everything. It was simply a matter of getting them there. That was the trouble with writing, the everyday string of events: you had to get them up in the morning and put them through their paces and serve them lunch, then put them to bed. All this to suspend disbelief, that was the first thing she'd learned.

The novelist must suspend disbelief, but then so must the nonfiction writer and sometimes she thought that must be even more difficult because truth was so unbelievable.

★   ★

Doria looked shocked, her eyes widened in disbelief. "Greg's gone? Gone where?"

I knew my voice was going wobbly. "We had a quarrel. The first in—such a long time. I'm out of practice, I guess. I let it get to me and said some awful things. Anyway, he packed a bag and left. In the middle of the night. Walking. Can you imagine that? I don't know where he would have gone. At first I thought to you and Allan with the classic pitch —my wife's thrown me out, may I sleep on your sofa? But he didn't, did he?"

"He could be staying with anybody." Doria answered warily, I thought. There was something else she wanted to say, but probably wouldn't. Friends don't say some things. Such as: What were you quarreling about? Such as: He's been acting peculiar ever since we found Pauline's body. Such as: The police will wonder where he's gone, and why.

I turned away and lit a cigarette. "Well," I said, "I'm not even looking for him. If he wants to come back, he can come back. But I'm not begging."

"Oh, Susan." She sighed. "I'll ask around."

"Tell him what I said."

"Yes, I'll tell him."

I watched her drive away in her red Skoda. She was upset and anxious to find him. I was anxious, too, but there wasn't anything I could do that wouldn't make matters worse. How, I wondered, did grown-up people get into such situations? If, on my wedding day, some uninvited wicked fairy had told me that this would happen to Greg and me, I would have never believed, never, never. . . .

I opened the shop and kept myself busy, working hard. When I wasn't attending customers, I was out back cutting out shirts and dresses for the seamstresses. I cut enough for a week, I guess. I was extra pleasant to everyone; I had to be. If I relaxed for a moment, I'd scream.

The gendarmes came just after closing time. I was almost glad to see them; I didn't enjoy being alone. They had a man with them, a small dark-haired mustached fellow who looked vaguely familiar. He was, they said, Monsieur Bagdonio of Puerto Rico, *vendeur de bijouterie.*

Yes, I said, I remembered him. He came selling jewelry in the spring. I'd bought some earrings and bracelets from him.

And a gold chain for the chic madame to wear avec bikini?

I answered carefully. He'd offered the chains, I told them, but I'd refused. I didn't think they would sell.

Little Mr. Bagdonio looked distressed, and muttered something in Spanish. I got the word *esposo* before I told him, "My Spanish is worse than my French. Please speak English to me."

He held his hands out to his sides. "Your husband, he thought you should try one to see. He bought a sample. One." He stared down at the floor. "It is very like the one I saw at the gendarmerie." He shrugged. "I cannot say it is the same, Señora, but it is very like."

I tried to keep my voice level. "It's possible." I couldn't call him a liar—what good would that do? "I don't know. I was busy with a customer, I just stopped long enough to look at what he was selling, to say yes or no. Greg, my husband, made the order and paid him." I'd spoken in English, I wasn't sure I could properly state it in French. "Martha," I called my maid from upstairs. "Would you kindly come down and translate."

She told them what I'd said. Gendarme Denhez, our friend André, turned into a cool-faced official, asked her a question, something about seeing *la chaîne.* "*Non, monsieur, je n'ai pas vu la chaîne.*"

André turned to me. My husband could have purchased the chain as a gift, *c'est possible?*

He didn't give it to me, I told him. *C'est possible* that Monsieur Bagdonio was mistaken? That he thought he'd left a chain, but hadn't? I hadn't seen the chain, Martha hadn't seen the chain, he could ask Lucillia or Marie, my seamstresses, he could ask Margaret who helped out in the shop.

And Monsieur Brady? Would it not be better to ask Monsieur Brady?

"*Monsieur Brady n'est pas ici.*"

"*Où est Monsieur Brady?*"

"*Je ne sais pas.*"

André raised handsome eyebrows. Madame did not know where her husband was? Madame did not. Madame regrets, but Madame could not tell him where to find her husband. He was somewhere on the island, but she simply could not say where.

They left then, hurrying, and I could imagine that the word would go out. Bring in Greg Brady for questioning. Oh, Greg, how did it ever come to this? Everything had been fine until the advent of Pauline.

★   ★

"You're not asleep, are you? Sitting there in that chair?"

Constance extracted herself from Susan's mind, blinking up into the light that shone from the doorway. "Oh, Jerry. I was writing. In my head. The bridge game all over?"

"Horace and Ed have gone to bed. Ruth's doing something out in the kitchen. How about a nightcap?"

Did she need another drink? How many had she had? Never mind, she'd have another. "Sure." She extended her glass. "Brandy, please. Not too much."

He went and returned quickly with two brandies. Seating himself on the chaise next to her, he sipped and allowed it was a beautiful night. "So peaceful here," he said, wistfully, she thought.

"Yes. Maybe too peaceful."

"For some."

"Are you thinking about living over here?" She'd miss him, she realized. He was such a gentle man. Sweet. Awful word for a man, but it so suited him.

"Thinking about it."

"Getting away from the place where you got away from it all?" What about that sentence structure? She must be a little bit tight.

"Like the man in the mirror reflected in the mirror reflected in the mirror? Yes, I suppose so. Doesn't sound healthy, does it?" She could see his teeth flash in the faint light.

She drank. "You want to get in. I think I want to get out."

"You should talk to Alfie about that. Alfie is wild to get out. He says we could change places." He laughed softly. "I could sit on Alfie's knee and he'd think up things to say."

Constance could understand that. Didn't she let her characters speak for her sometimes? Or was that what he meant? She was too tired and too fuzzy to follow it through. "I will speak to Alfie," she said. "I'll tell him my dreams, and he can tell me his." She began to hum the old song.

"Oh, you can talk to him now if you want to."

"Alfie is here?"

"Of course. Wherever I goeth, so goeth Alfie. He's in bed now, I think, but probably not asleep, he never goes to sleep until I get in. Come on." He pushed himself out of the chaise. "We'll take the bottle of brandy and Alfie can join the party." He reached out a hand to help her up.

"Why not?" asked Constance, giggling. Giggling, she thought. Silly woman. Sad silly old woman. What in the name of God was she doing here? Walking hand in hand with a man and a bottle up a dark path in a strange place beside a devious sea?

"You know I've had too much to drink, don't you, Jerry?"

"Maybe a wee drop, Constance. Not too much too much, just a little."

"I should be ashamed of myself. At my age I should know better—"

"I wish you'd stop referring to your age. You're not an old woman, but you sound that way when you talk like that."

"I'm fifty years old, accent on the old. I'm not kidding myself."

"You're a fine looking blonde lady."

She felt the old familiar warmth that admiration could bring, and pushed it away. "I don't mind looking older, but what scares me is the mind. I'm a writer, but I don't know if I can write anymore. The—the new books I order from the States—I don't understand why but they're all the same. Somebody goes on about his/her and everybody else's sex problems, ad nauseam." She pushed a strand of hair out of her eyes and leaned forward. "Please tell me, Jerry, is everybody like that inside their heads? If all they think of is sex, how does anything get done in the world?"

He peered at her through his glass. "I'm the wrong one to ask, Connie." He grinned. "I'm a celibate."

"Don't joke, Jerry. I'm really scared. When I was thirteen, maybe fourteen, I knew all, or at least most all the words. I remember one evening I was in the city park with my girl friend and her boy friend. I was a kind of fifth wheel there (see, I am drunk, how can a third person be a fifth wheel?). All of us got—feisty is my word, a word you don't see any more, even my words are old. I shouted all the shockers I knew into the park, and then I felt silly. I don't need those words. I know what they mean and I know a lot of people talk that way but you don't—hardly anyone I know does." She laughed. "We used to think it bad manners. We used to shine up our words along with our faces. But now . . ." She sat back feeling as foolish as that long-ago night in the park.

"The contention . . ." He had trouble with that word, he must have been a little drunk, too. "The contention is that if we use one set of phrases in our minds and another in our speech, we are hypocrites. The 'let it all hang out' school despises hypocrisy, deplores sham; they alone are the arbiters of fakery and it is their considered opinion that all except themselves are fakes." He blinked. "How's that for a speech? I'd better leave the talking to Alfie." He reached for the dummy who sat against the headboard of the bed and sat him properly in his lap. "What do you think, Alfie, about the state of the world?"

And Alfie answered, "I think I shall tell you about the time I once goosed a ghost. You're supposed to ask, What did you get? And I say, A handful of sheet."

Constance laughed. It wasn't very funny but she laughed until she cried.

★   ★

Greg had vanished, it seemed. Simply vanished. No one admitted picking him up the night he left, no one admitted seeing him. Well, at first Harold Crozier had thought he'd seen Greg on Front Street in Philipsburg the next morning, but after he thought it over he was certain it had been the day before. Greg had not left Juliana Airport by plane, neither had he left via Esperance on the French side. So, unless he was hiding out somewhere on the island, he could only have gotten off by boat. The gendarmes and the Dutch police were still questioning all the small boat owners in such places as Simpson Bay and French Cul de Sac and Sandy Ground. But, so far, after eight days of wondering and waiting on my part, Greg had simply vanished.

Yes, I'd finally told the gendarmes, we had quarreled about Pauline Gray. Yes, my husband had been attracted to her. No, I could not swear where he'd been the day, the night she was killed. I just couldn't be sure, I couldn't remember what we'd done that day, it had been a day like any other day.

It was clear now that they believed he had killed her, although they didn't tell me that in so many words. And everybody else thought so too. They treated me with exquisite kindness, especially Doria and Allan who kept asking me to dinner and kept dropping in night and day. And I looked into her sapphire eyes and got a message: She was relieved, so relieved, because Allan, too, had been lured (had he taken the bait?) and now he was safe and she felt a little guilty for being so relieved.

I didn't blame her.

On the ninth day, Brett Carlisle passed by and commiserated without referring at all to Greg. "You and I are going out tonight," he announced. "It's time you sinned just a little. We'll go to the casino and lose our shirts. How's that for living dangerously?"

"I'm not going anywhere," I snapped. "Except to bed." And nastily I added, "Alone."

"Ah, Susan, don't be difficult. And don't be ridiculous. My motives are strictly nonulterior. I'm feeling neglected and I want to go on the town with a pretty, bitchy lady."

"What's wrong with Gillian?"

"She's not half bitchy enough."

I couldn't help it, I had to smile. No two ways about it, he could make me feel better whether I wanted to or not. But I wasn't going to any casino with Brett Carlisle. "I hate casinos. I know nothing about gambling. I hate to lose money. And what would people say? You know that Greg has left me."

"More fool he. Besides, that's what I love about you. You don't really care about what people say."

"Of course I do! I'm an upright, rigid, restricted lady and will be till I die, if it kills me."

He threw back his handsome head and laughed. "Susan, luv, you are something. Don't you know I can see straight through people? Don't you know that's my talent, my one and only talent? You and I are two of a kind. I call us the victims of the Chinese curse."

"What Chinese curse?"

"The one that goes: Be careful of what you wish for, you may get it."

Too bad, I thought, that I wasn't what he thought I was. He was exactly the kind of man I would have wanted, had I been the kind of woman a part of me longed to be. "Your see-all eye has cataracts," I told him. "I am not—repeat, not—going to any casino with you. I've only been once in my life and then as an onlooker. I don't even know how to behave. And I have no intention of throwing my money away in some kind of stupid gesture just to show the world I don't care."

"See—you don't give a damn about what people think. We'll play twenty-one. Blackjack. It's the game where you have the best chance."

"Brett, no! I don't know how to play twenty-one or blackjack or whatever it's called. I mean, I know how it's played but I don't know how to play it—there's a difference, you know. And besides that I don't want to go out with anybody. Especially you!"

Brett grinned. I was doing my best to be disagreeable and he was enjoying it. "I'll put it on paper for you. You can memorize it or slip it up your sleeve or, in case you're sleeveless, down your bosom."

Brett smiled the smile that made him a neat fortune. "We'll have a good time, Susan. Look out, Little Bay, here comes the dynamic duo!"

After I'd talked myself into it, I went as I'd promised, all out. I picked out the fanciest, flossiest long dress in the shop and shortened it. I washed my hair and dried it with the blow dryer which I seldom took time to use. I put on makeup—eye shadow, mascara, the whole bit. When I looked into the mirror, I realized I hadn't gone to this much trouble in a long time. Greg hadn't seemed to care. Greg had seemed to like me the way I was. Greg had seemed . . . to hell with Greg. (Oh, when would they find him? And then what?)

Brett, in trim white pants and black and white tucked and embroidered Guayabarra shirt, looked like the glamour boy he was. He whistled when he saw me and put a nasty glint in his eyes. "Maybe my motives are ulterior after all," he said. I grinned and answered, "Bug off."

We went out into the cooling evening where he waited while I locked the shop door. A voice from the shadows of the car said, "Good evening, Mrs. Brady," and I nearly jumped. Morry Bunty sat behind the wheel of Brett's Mercedes. I was immediately sorry I'd come.

"Morry's going to drop us," Brett told me, guiding me to the back seat. "Morry needs the car, he's got a date." Brett opened the door for me. "But he's being cosy about it. He won't say with whom."

"I thought maybe you'd gone," I told Bunty.

"Not yet," he replied, much more pleasantly than my almost-rudeness warranted.

"Morry can stay as long as he pleases." Brett slid in beside me and shut the door. "He likes it here, don't you, Morry?"

"It's paradise." He started the engine and drove off. I told myself I needn't worry about Morry Bunty anymore, the fat was in the fire, the fly was in the ointment, the monkey wrench was in the gears and the worst that was yet to come had come. Then I ran out of clichés and listened to Brett being charming. Not a bad way to spend an evening. Not bad at all.

There was a pretty good crowd at Little Bay for off-season, but then Little Bay always had a better than average occupancy rate, no matter what the time of year. When Greg and I had first visited St. Martin, Little Bay Beach Hotel had been small, only forty-six rooms formed in small connected cottage-type units on the hillside. Now they had two big modern wings along the beach itself and could accommodate over two hundred. Progress; but I felt a little nostalgic for the old days when things were easier and Greg and I had been . . . but I couldn't think about that. I had to smile. Be scintillating. I reminded myself that I was out with the idol of millions and he was all mine for the evening. What more did I want? What more indeed? Be careful of what you wish for, you might get it.

We saw people we knew among the tourists. We greeted one another and smiled and made small talk, nobody mentioned Greg at all and that's the way it can be on St. Martin. When everybody knows what's going on, or think they do, they have the good manners to keep silent about it.

We played blackjack. Brett won, I lost. Not much —twenty dollars maybe, and Brett said that was practically winning because we played for over two hours. I said I needed more time to study the number system he'd given me and he said, fine, we'd do it again. Then we went to the After Burner and had pizza and the music was very loud. Morry was with us again; he'd shown up at Little Bay just before we left. I'd had quite a bit to drink and I didn't mind his being along so much by that time. But I fussed at him because he was so quiet. "Don't you ever say anything?" I demanded.

"Not much." He smiled at me and his eel eyes gleamed.

"What shall we do next?" Brett wanted to know.

"Isn't it time to go home?" I couldn't read my watch too well, was it 2 A.M.? Funny, I didn't feel tired.

"I know," said Brett, "let's take the boat out."

"The boat? And go where?"

He shrugged. "Who cares? It's Saturday. You don't have to open for business again until Monday."

That struck me as funny. I hadn't been irresponsible in years and years. I laughed out loud. Who cared if I went out on a boat, any boat, and sailed someplace, anyplace. "Why not?" I asked when I'd stopped laughing.

"That's my Susan." Brett signaled the waiter, paid the check and hurried me out.

"But I haven't finished my drink."

"Bring it with you!"

I guess I knew Brett had a boat but I'd never seen it. What kind of boat was it? A rowboat? I began to snicker at the thought of rowing out to sea in a fancy dress and eye shadow. I could stand in the bow like George Washington crossing the Delaware. How were they going to take a boat out at two o'clock in the morning if it was two o'clock, what morning? Whoops, spilled my drink, mascara felt so heavy, dragging my eyelashes down and down, stay up eyelashes . . .

I woke up a little later. It couldn't have been too much later because it was still dark and every star in the universe was shining through a window at me. I was sitting in a chair and the floor beneath my feet was moving so it only took me a few minutes to realize I was on the boat and the boat was good-sized and the boat was moving.

I was by myself, but there were other people on board because I could hear them on deck. I tried to stand up and found I could do that all right. I looked around. I could see that the boat was solid and plush and expensive-looking. The place where I stood was, I realized, the saloon. Had I known nothing about boats I would have called it a living room because that's what it was fitted out as. I made my way to the door, a few steps up, a sliding glass door.

"Hey," I called.

Brett and Morry were sitting on a banquette, feet up on a table, heads back, drinks in hand. They stood up when they saw me; Brett came to get me.

"Where are we going?" I asked. There was the steady roar of a motor. I had to speak loudly to be heard above it.

"Ever been to St. Kitts?"

"No. How far by sea?"

"Quite a way. Maybe seventy nautical miles, something like that. Come sit. We'll sing sea chanteys."

I let him lead me. "Who's driving this thing?"

"I've got a skipper, Captain Mingo. We roused him from the sack. He was delighted. He lives with his wife and six children. Wouldn't you be glad to get away from your wife and six children, Morry?"

"You bet." He moved over so I could sit down.

"What kind of boat is this?"

"A Bertram."

"What's its name?"

"*Ondine.* How are you feeling?"

"Fine." I hiccuped. "I'm feeling fine."

"What you need is a drink."

Maybe I did. Very good for hiccups. I hadn't had the hiccups in years. But what did I want to drink?

Ugh. Whatever I'd been drinking tasted lousy. "I'll have . . . have you got any Pernod?" I'd read about that someplace. Hemingway?

Brett grinned. "Pernod? You're getting esoteric, aren't you, luv?"

"Exotic." *Hic.*

"I'll see if we've got some." He disappeared into the saloon.

Morry Bunty stood up and stretched. "I think," he said, "I'll hit the sack."

"Sweet dreams." I had to spoil it with another *hic.*

"Don't let the bedbugs bite." He passed Brett coming back with bottle and glass. Taking the glass, I smelled—wasn't sure I like the smell; tasted, licorice. I leaned back, glass in hand.

I woke up with a very bad headache, and a sense of something wrong.

I was lying—fully clothed—on a narrow bunk. Where, I wondered, and then remembered. Brett's boat.

We weren't moving. I couldn't see out.

I swung my legs off the bunk. Oh, God. The headache. I had to have air.

I staggered to my feet. I called, "Brett." It came out a croak.

I saw a doorway ahead and aimed for it. I was in the saloon.

I made my way to the deck in fits and starts, grabbing here, grabbing there. The sun was fearful. "Brett!"

I shielded my eyes and looked around. Wherever I was, I'd never been there before in my life.

We were tied alongside a wooden dock that led to a beach fringed by a double row of palm trees. Beyond the palms was a lawn, a very large lawn, most unusual for the Caribbean, the kind of lawn one mowed from a riding mower. Tastefully placed on the lawn were two low white buildings. I couldn't see too clearly what with my headache and all but the whole place looked deserted.

I shouted, "Brett!" and held my ears. I shouldn't have done that. I closed my eyes. The sun was so bright. The boat moved slightly and I thought, I'm going to be sick. Better get off the boat to be sick. Could I? Get from deck to dock? . . . I got to the gunwale. It was going up and down; the dock was standing still. I knelt, turned backwards, clung to the gunwale, put one foot over . . . this wasn't going to work . . .

Somebody grabbed me and set me upright on solid dock. Morry Bunty said, "You okay?"

I couldn't answer. I turned away from him and threw up into the ocean.

★   ★

There was the sound of a car in the driveway. "Damn," said Constance. Agnes was back.

"Where were you all weekend?" Agnes demanded from the top step of the veranda.

The preferred reply would have been "None of your business," but Constance refrained. Agnes probably knew anyway. "I went to Anguilla."

"Oh, really?" Oh, yes, she'd heard. "Where'd you stay?"

Constance told her.

"Then you must have run into Horace and Ed."

"Yes, they were there."

"Horace is very upset about Anguilla."

"Why would Horace be upset about Anguilla?" Good heavens, thought Constance, I'm playing straight man to Agnes—games?

"He's keen on buying land there, didn't he tell you?"

"I guess he mentioned it." She supposed it had come up but with all that conversation about running from one official to another, she hadn't paid much attention.

"He wants to put a television station over there, to tie it up with the present Saba–St. Martin station. He says it will be the most powerful one in the Caribbean. But he's run into all kinds of difficulties, some of it because of Bootsie Baker."

"Bootsie? What did she have to do with it?"

"Well, when he started he ran into some opposition there. He says they act like he wants to take over the island when all he wants is to provide first-rate entertainment. Well, anyway, he got Bootsie to go over and buy some land as, what do you call it, a straw?"

Constance nodded.

"And now he can't find the papers. He's just wild." Agnes sat in the wicker chair with a pleased expression (the wicker chair complained).

"Do you think they were stolen? That could explain the murder."

Agnes smiled patronizingly. "Oh, Connie, you do have murder on your mind. I suppose it's an occupational hazard. Horace says they've decided Bootsie wasn't murdered at all."

"Then what was she doing over there—alone? How did she get there? And how did she drown, such a good swimmer?"

"Oh, didn't you know? They found her boat. It slipped its anchor or whatever they call it and drifted, they found it on the rocks at St. Barts. Apparently she took it over, went swimming and bingo—maybe a heart attack?

Horace thinks it must have been. The big mystery is what she did with all those important papers. He's looked everywhere, but nothing."

"So that's why he handled the funeral arrangements."

"Well, maybe. But out of the goodness of his heart, too. Horace is a very kind man."

St. Barts. Would a boat drift from Shoal Bay to St. Barts? She was being ridiculous. Agnes, for once, was no doubt right. Besides, Constance had other problems to worry about. Greg had disappeared and she'd left Susan alone on St. Kitts with Brett and Morry. Living dangerously, that's what she was doing; what did she really know about Brett and his friend . . . or about Jerry Tosca, for that matter?

Stop it! Jerry Tosca had nothing to do with the book or anything else.

★ ★

"Green monkeys! Honest to God, green monkeys, Brett!" I was lying on the chaise, getting some sun, and they ran by, a bunch of them. "Where do you suppose they came from?"

We were in the main house. Brett was tending bar in the late afternoon. There was no one else there. Brett had keys. He explained that friends of his owned the place, had given him carte blanche whenever he wanted to stay a few days.

"They say the French brought the great-great-great granddaddy monkeys (and grandmas, of course) centuries ago as pets. When the French left, the monkeys took off for the hills. Now I'm told they number in the thousands but nobody knows for sure. Here you are, Susan, the hair of the dog."

I accepted my drink thankfully; I'd spent most of

the day sleeping, it had been years since I'd slept so
long, I'd gone out like a light.

I shook my head. "I thought I was hallucinating."

"No way. Here you are, Morry. There's a Behav-
ioral Science Foundation at a place called Estridge
where they study the little beasts."

"What's the island across the bay?"

"Nevis. Want to go over tomorrow?"

"Of course not! You said we'd go back. I have to
open the shop in the morning!" I put my gin and
tonic down hard. "Come on. You promised. Let's not
play games." I looked at Morry, who sat unob-
trusively in the corner, ubiquitous Morry, always
there—but easy to ignore. He blended into the back-
ground, damn him. No doubt that made him the
complete detective.

"Didn't he promise, Morry? You heard him?"

Brett laughed. "Simmer down, Susan. I'll take you
home. You sound like sweet sixteen out on her first
date with the dude in the big convertible. But you
can't deny you're feeling better. You're looking better, that's for sure. Every so often we all have to get
off our rock."

"I have to feel better," I confessed. "If I'd felt any
worse, I'd have died. And you're right about sweet
sixteen—I haven't had such a hangover since I was a
callow youth. I'm ashamed of myself."

"Don't be. You needed to unwind. Here's to
Morry." He raised his glass. "Morry, the chef. He's
going to cook our dinner, aren't you, Morry? We
found some tournedos in the freezer and a frozen

macaroni and cheese. Not bad for a deserted island, eh, Morry?"

I thought I'd better offer. "I'll cook if you like, Morry."

Brett laughed. "Nonsense. Morry insists on doing all sorts of little things for me. He's got this proud idea that he's paying his way, right, Morry?"

Eel-eyes glittered. "Right, Brett." He stood up. "I'd better get at it." And he vanished into the kitchen, a little like the Cheshire cat, I thought; only his grin was left.

I picked up my drink again, a nice mild gin and tonic, it tasted good. I wondered what sort of little things Morry did for Brett. Paying one's way with a living legend (magazines still carried stories about the last of the great leading men, reminding the world of his various wives, his starring roles, his legions of devoted fans) must be a tough number.

"Do you want to talk about it?" asked Brett.

I took a long swallow. "No." I stared at him. He was a beautiful man. "Yes. I guess so." I looked down at my glass. "Where do I begin?"

"Anywhere. At the beginning?"

My ice cubes were melting. "Could I have some more ice, please?"

"Here, let me freshen it."

"We married young. I was—maybe too young. I'd been accepted at Wellesley and was due to go that fall. Greg was at Boston University, he'd been to Korea but now he was back working for his bachelor's—Phys. Ed. He wanted to coach. Greg was a jock before they were called jocks. Thanks." I accepted my drink.

"We decided we couldn't live without each other. My family was furious (the Wellesley acceptance included a scholarship) but I was the kind of only child who couldn't be reasoned with. Greg's mother was dead and his father had his own problems—so, we went ahead and did it." I tried to smile. "Actually it didn't turn out too badly." I let the smile go. "Until now."

"No children?"

I shook my head. I didn't want to go into that. The truth of the matter was that I'd had my hands full bringing up Greg, but I wouldn't say that to anyone. "Greg quit college to go to work for his father. His father was a clothing manufacturer, but, he died after we came down here. Greg hated it, I realized that almost right away, but he stuck it out as long as he could and I worked, too, at various things until we could save enough to get away. And when we could, we did. We came to St. Martin and opened up the shop and lived happily ever after." I blinked away tears. "Almost." Brave smile.

"They made a movie along those lines." Brett's eyes were kind. "Called it *Love Story.*"

I swallowed hard; I had to stop before I started blubbering. "Maybe I'd better give Morry a hand."

"Why do you think he left? Did he say he was leaving?" He leaned forward, eyes compelling. "You need to talk about this, Susan. Tell me."

"He said he was leaving. I was angry. I said I didn't care. I said maybe we'd both be better off. I was frightened, that's why I was angry." I felt mes- merized. I was the heroine in a Brett Carlisle movie. I was watching myself up there on a big screen act- ing the heroine.

"Did he take clothes? Money? His passport?"

I nodded. "That's when I thought—I knew he meant it."

"Where? He didn't say where?"

"No. Don't you think I'd have gone after him if I knew where?"

"Then, why? People have arguments all the time— every woman I ever had anything to do with—you must have argued before. Why did he disappear?"

He was pushing. The script writer had given him the power—she had to answer, to speak her lines.

"Because they thought he killed her. Because he thought I thought he killed her." I was almost breathless, the words had to be pushed out.

"Do you think he killed Pauline?"

"I don't know!" I had to cry now, I couldn't help it.

He let me. After a little he gave me a handkerchief and whispered, "It's all right, Susan. I'm sorry, but you had to let it out."

I blew my nose. "I offered to lie. I told him I would swear he was with me. He said that was no good, other people had seen me alone that day. He was afraid, too."

"Where was he that day?"

"He picked up a shipment from John King. He did some errands. The usual chores."

"Then other people saw him, too."

"Yes, but all they'll remember is that he was out in the car. He could have driven to meet her, he could have gone with her—there's just no way to prove that he couldn't have!"

"Yes, but there's no way to prove that he did."

I told him about the chain then.

He thought about it. "That's no proof either. The jewelry salesman could have been mistaken. The chain could have gotten into someone else's hands."

"We didn't sell it."

"Somebody could have just picked it up, a shoplifter, anybody."

I stared at him through blurred eyes. "You make it sound—better for him."

"That's what I'm trying to do."

"Why?"

"Because I don't think Greg is guilty."

I took a deep breath. "Thank you. But, you see, everybody else does. I can tell—Doria, Allan, everybody. Especially now that he's run away."

"Yes, that wasn't very smart."

"No. Oh, Brett! I don't know what to do. I can't find him, I don't know where to look."

"I just remembered something." Morry Bunty's voice came from the kitchen, he must have been listening. "I wonder if anybody's checked Pauline Gray's place."

Brett stood up. "Of course!" he said.

"If I was going to hide out, I'd figure that might be the best place. At least until I'd made better arrangements." Morry came to the kitchen door, he had an apron tied round his waist and a big fork in his hand. "And now that I think of it, I remember I heard a car that night on the road to your house, Brett, and that same road goes to the Gray place. I heard it in my sleep and I thought, wonder where it's going this time of night, and then I didn't hear it anymore so I forgot it." He waved the fork. "As soon as we get back . . ."

"Right." Brett swallowed the rest of his drink. "Dinner about ready?"

"In a minute." Morry disappeared.

"But, Brett . . ."

"Yes, luv?"

"Whose car? He didn't take a car."

"Maybe the murderer gave him a lift."

"The murderer! Why? How?"

"I don't know how but I know why. With Greg gone, everybody—as you said—would assume they knew just who killed Pauline Gray."

I jumped up. "Hurry, Morry. Let's get back to St. Martin. Oh, Brett, if he's only there, if he's only all right . . . Oh, Brett. My God, I'm such a fool."

Pauline's house. I shivered. Anybody could hide there, I thought. There is no color more unattractive than the color of raw cement. Ugly, rambling wall hiding ugly little square buildings.

The house itself was shuttered and locked but Morry seemed to have a key. Brett chuckled at my expression. "We didn't steal it," he said, "we borrowed it."

The door creaked as it opened. Wouldn't it just, I thought. I wanted to yell "Greg" into the musty darkness but I was afraid of—I didn't know what I was afraid of.

The light switch didn't bring forth light—power off, no doubt—so Morry bumbled into the blackness and opened shutters.

I made a noise, not a scream, more of a squeak. A

rat disappeared into the darkness of the next room. "Somebody's been here," I ventured.

Cushions had been pulled off a wicker couch. A small table lay on its side, the lamp which had rested upon it was broken, paperback books were tumbled in a heap from a bookcase. There were no chairs—surely she had had chairs. "Somebody's been here," I repeated.

"Yes." Brett picked up the table and lamp. "Her stereo's missing. Unless it's in the bedroom. And some chairs. I'd guess somebody's helped themselves."

I widened my eyes at him. "Not Greg?"

"Not unless he's furnishing a new nest somewhere."

Morry had gone into the next room; we followed. Clothes and bedding were strewn over the bedroom, a pair of empty liquor bottles on the kitchen counter along with three used glasses. Cupboards seemed oddly empty; Brett thought that dishes and canned goods had disappeared. "Along with the rest of the liquor supply," he surmised.

"Don't touch the glasses," Morry warned us. "They should have fingerprints, the Dutch cops will want those."

"I don't think Greg has been here," I said forlornly.

"How can you be sure?" asked Morry.

"He wouldn't have done this."

"He might have been here before—or after."

I shook my head. "I don't know why I ever thought he might come here. It isn't like him."

Brett cocked an eyebrow. "Running off wasn't like him either, was it?"

"No. Let's go. I don't like this place."

"Come, Morry." It was almost as though he snapped his fingers to command his man. "Let's go up to our place and have breakfast."

"I've got to get back to Grand Case," I reminded him.

"You've got time for breakfast." He shut the door behind us, and the sun seemed extra bright after the gloom inside. I looked up to Brett's house high on the side of the hill above us. Three houses, main building, two bedroom suites, four really if you counted "Fort Marion" as he called it, a crenellated block that housed the cisterns, his water supply. I wondered why he'd called it Marion. A lady he'd loved? Brett didn't seem the sentimental type to me, but then how well did I really know him? Not well at all.

★　　★

Master Alfie Tosca
requests the company
of Madame Constance Cobble
at dinner
on Wednesday at seven o'clock
at the home of M. Jerald Tosca
The Lowlands, St. Martin
Repondez oui s'il vous plaît!
(*Pas non*)

The invitation was printed in a childish hand with a felt-tip pen on the back of a glossy photo of Jerry and Alfie. The picture was autographed on the front in bold masculine writing: *to Constance with love, Jerry.* Underneath that was more printing: *and Alfie, too.*

The publicity photo had been taken some years before, Constance decided. Jerry's hair was cut short in the style of the fifties and he wore a tuxedo. He looked very young, almost pretty. Alfie looked like Alfie except that now he was usually dressed in a Heineken beer tee shirt and blue jeans while in the picture he wore a traditional suit with a fancy vest.

A dinner party. She avoided many of the Lowland soirees, pleading the pressures of work as an excuse, but in this case—well, she'd have to go, although she wasn't sure why. She felt an inexplicable urge to go to his side when beckoned; it was almost as though he gave an unheard call for help that she alone heard. Oh, what nonsense. Jerry Tosca was a rather wistful shadow of a once well-known man and all she felt was sympathy. Better get back to writing, she thought. If your heroines are foolish enough to think such thoughts, so be it, but you . . . !

Antoine, face and fingers smudged with traces of blue and yellow paint, looked at me with sad saint-like eyes. "You have had no word from Greg?" he asked.

I shook my head.

He glanced away—in embarrassment? "I had a dream." He shot a quick look at me. "In my dreams I sometimes find answers, or what I perceive to be answers."

I touched his muscular arm in supplication. "You dreamed of Greg?"

Now he nodded. His expression changed. I read compassion, concern, doubt. "Sometimes my dreams are not the true answer."

"You dreamed he is—you dreamed that something has happened to him."

Antoine frowned. "I saw a large body of water. It was—like a cinema when the camera starts way back and then moves in closer until something that is just a little speck in the beginning gets larger and larger. I couldn't tell what the speck was at first, the speck in the water, but at last I made it out. It was a body—a man's body floating face down in the water."

It was hard to move my lips. "Greg?"

"It seemed so." Antoine picked up one of my hands and held it. "I wondered if I should tell you but then I thought, I must."

I felt ill. Words from a self-made mystic, a picture drawn in thin air. "It can't be. He's such a good swimmer." An automatic protestation. "You don't think—he wouldn't, he wouldn't kill himself!"

Antoine shook his unkempt head in a gesture of uncertainty. "Only he can answer that." He let go of my hand. "I'm sorry. Believe me, Susan, I am very sorry."

I blinked rapidly, licking my dry lips. "No," I said loudly. "No. I don't believe you. I don't believe your dream means anything!"

"Perhaps not."

A skinny little man in cut-off shorts, rubber sandals, dirty feet. What did he know? Nothing. Here I was, stomach churning, face hot, hands cold, all because of this . . . this . . . Caribbean pseudovisionary. "It isn't true," I whispered. The woodenness had left my lips, now they trembled. "Greg isn't dead."

Antoine didn't speak. Then he made a small bow and walked out the door. I had to sit down, I had to compose myself, it was almost time to open the shop.

But how could I when I felt so terrible? Breathe deeply, I told myself. You know how these people are, some of them. They still believe in obeah, jumbies and evil spells. Antoine, as intelligent as he is, is a throwback.

"Susan! Are you there?" Doria stuck her bright dandelion head in the door. "What's the matter?" She hurried toward me. "Have they found Greg?"

"No. I—I'm just having a delayed reaction, I guess." I tried to smile, but my mouth didn't want to turn up.

"I've been so worried about you. I've been here two or three times. Where have you been?"

"I had to get away. I took a boat trip."

Her eyebrows rose. "A boat trip? Where?"

What she meant was, with whom. I hoped she'd understand, I hadn't thought about explaining when I'd gone. "I was . . . going crazy. No word, no sign. I couldn't stand it. I went to St. Kitts with Brett on his boat."

She tried to hide her reaction. "To St. Kitts? Oh, really?"

My voice grew shrill. "My honor is safe, don't worry. Morry Bunty played chaperon."

She laughed lightly. "Oh, Susan, I *know* you, I didn't think that at all." She sobered instantly. "It's been days since he vanished. I've tried to put myself in your place—I just don't know what I'd do."

I stared at my hands, they were holding tight to one another. "Antoine dreamed he was dead." I looked up at her and saw that sudden tears gleamed in her eyes. "You think so, too."

"No! Of course not. It's just that—you'd think there'd be some word. How can he torture you like this? It isn't like him, he's always seemed so considerate." She touched my shoulder. "That's what worries us so."

True, he was considerate. An ideal husband except that I was left making all the decisions. Well, that's what I wanted, wasn't it? That was my nature. And yet underneath that constant giving in, tacit acknowledgment of my authority, resentment must exist. I would have resented him if he'd run my life. Untrue—I didn't run his life. Ooh, Susan, you lie. You did, you know you did.

Doria was saying something, and I knew I should listen. ". . . come to dinner tonight. Allan went fishing yesterday morning and caught some grouper."

I didn't want to go anywhere. I just wanted to sit by myself and talk myself into ease of mind. "What time?"

"Six-thirty? Seven? As soon as you can." She hugged me. A car braked outside, customers. Doria left and the customers came in and stared at the clothes on the racks and the handmade gifts on the shelves. I made my little speech, "We make clothes here; we offer, also, clothes made on nearby islands. Look around and call if you need help."

They wandered around, hangers clicked on the rods as the woman pushed dresses aside. "Where are you from?" asked the man.

"The Boston area."

"You live here?"

"Yes."

"How long have you lived here?"

"Six years."

Now the clincher was due (I'd thought of making a recording). I got it: "Do you like it?"

How many times I'd thought to say, sarcastically of course, "No, I hate it. But I can't go back to the States, I'm wanted for armed robbery."

Instead, the polite response (true until last week): "I love it."

They wandered around some more, buying one postcard before leaving.

Doria and Allan operated the Cove Inn, six suites right on the water. They lived in the main building that housed also the bar, the dining room and the kitchen. When I arrived shortly after seven, Allan was behind the bar serving drinks to four guests and Doria was in the kitchen settling something with Madyline, the cook.

"Hi, Susan. Mr. and Mrs. Cobine, this is Susan Brady. She owns a shop in Grand Case, the *Fleur de Lis*, maybe you've seen it."

Mrs. Cobine, a big-busted fluffy blonde, bounced on her bar stool. "Oh, Charles, I wanted to go in, remember, and you said we had to get back for your tennis date. You've simply got to take me back there."

Mr. Cobine looked ceilingward. "My wife is always shopping. She shops to come here and after she gets here, what does she want to do? Go shopping!"

"Oh, Charles!" Mrs. Cobine tickled him in the ribs. "You know you don't mean it." He giggled and they gazed into each other's eyes and, thank heavens, Gillian Sparrow came in and I had someone I liked to talk to.

"Susan!" She kissed my cheek. "Forgive me, I've been meaning to get over to see you."

"You're forgiven," I said. I hoped she wouldn't mention Greg. I couldn't bear to explain to the Cobines. She didn't say anything but her eyes said, "I'm so sorry." I felt like a grieving widow.

"I thought Brett and Morry would be here by now," she said to Allan.

"Not yet. What will you have to drink?"

Brett and Morry were coming, too? Doria must have planned quite a little gathering. Suddenly I was frightened by it all. I felt hemmed in. I wished I were able to pack a bag and run somewhere. But I couldn't, of course. I couldn't go anywhere until Greg was found. I could only smile at Allan and say sweetly, "Gin and tonic, please. With a lime?"

★　★

Constance returned from driving her maid home to find Horace Albertson at her desk, reading her manuscript. "Very interesting," he said before she could open her mouth. "You've turned Bootsie into Pauline Gray."

"Please put that down." She was furious. She never permitted anyone to read an unfinished work.

"Come on. Now, Constance." Horace shook his head. A lock of his rather long, thick hair fell forward, giving him an unexpected boyish look. "You're writing to be read, aren't you? It's not as though I'm reading your mail."

"It isn't finished."

He grinned. "I can see that." He put the sheaf of pages down. "Who done it?"

She made a gesture of impatience.

Horace put on a bland look. "Sorry if I irritated you. I wish you'd finish the thing. Maybe then I could find out where Bootsie left her valuable papers. Seems they're missing and since some of them pertained to me, I'm—pardon the expression—pissed off."

"What do you want, Horace? I'm going out to dinner and I need to get ready."

"Oh, I came with an invitation. Cleo James begged me to intercede for her. She's anxious to have you on her TV show."

"Oh, yes, she spoke to me about it. She was vague about dates; I was vague about my answer. I don't like publicity much."

Horace, lighting a cigarette, grinned again. "I can understand that." Constance frowned. Horace was a man who broke rules, she thought. You weren't supposed to refer to past tragedies.

"It would help the girl," Horace continued. "It's not easy to stage a good TV show locally. I told her you were a kind, generous person, that I knew you wouldn't refuse. What would it cost you? A few minutes of your time."

"When? What do I do?" I figured I should do it and get it over with; few people I knew listened anyway. Horace should concentrate more on his existing business rather than looking for expansion. The rumor was that the TV station had money problems.

"This Saturday. She'll tape at ten so you get there say, nine-thirty. She asks that you bring a list of questions you think would be helpful."

Ah, well. If Constance planned the questions, there'd be no chance of the interview taking off in the wrong direction. "All right. Tell her all right." An afterthought: "What should I wear?"

Horace shrugged. "Whatever you want. You always

look good." When he smiled he reminded her of—what? A used car salesman?

He came toward her. "Well, if you aren't going to invite me for a drink, I'll run along. I've got to stop and see Jerry Tosca anyway."

"Jerry? What for?"

"Now, you aren't the only celebrity on this island, are you? Cleo wants Jerry on her show, too."

"Messenger is a strange role for you, isn't it, Horace?"

"Oh, I've got to see Jerry on another matter so I told Cleo as long as I was in the neighborhood, I'd drop in. So long, Constance. Hurry up and finish that book. I want to find out who killed Bootsie Baker."

"It isn't about Bootsie Baker. My characters are strictly fictional. Bootsie's death was a mere coincidence."

He stopped directly in front of her, put his hands up in mock defense. "I believe you, Connie. I believe you." He gave her a swift kiss on the cheek and left. For a big man he made very little noise on the stairs; he'd been wearing rubber thong sandals. Jerry's party was at seven —he'd probably be annoyed at Horace's premature appearance. No, Jerry seldom seemed to be annoyed. She wondered who was coming; no one had said anything, but then she'd not seen many people of late. Even Agnes had left her alone with the result that she had gotten some work done. Not that she was especially pleased with the work in progress. Something was tugging her sleeve, holding her back. The coincidence of the death of Bootsie Baker? When her story reached its end, with the murderer named, what if the fictional killer had a nonfictional counterpart? Connie's killer, an arbitrary choice based upon the rules of the game. The murderer of

Bootsie Baker? Constance had no idea, no opinion; she disliked true crime and found it impossible to write about it. She'd been asked if such and such really happened. She'd answered, always, honestly, no, I made it up. Writing about death and violence was only fun when it was imaginary.

She decided to wear her favorite long dress, not a new one but one she hadn't worn in some time. Actually, she'd begun to think it was too young for her, being white, with bare shoulders, snug bodice and embroidered skirt. Still, the mirror told her it looked well and tonight she felt—defiant.

The long driveway leading to Jerry's house was lit by candles in sand-filled paper bags (had he been reading her manuscript, too?). Holding her skirt out of the sand, she walked across the parking area—funny that there were no other cars, perhaps she was early. Jerry's Datsun was parked by the small detached guest house. Well, she was the first to arrive, it seemed. She walked around the side of the house to the front which faced the sea. She called, "Hi—anybody home?"

Handsome amber hurricane lamps burned with a soft glow. A huge bouquet of scarlet bougainvillea and creamy hibiscus filled the center of a low table; behind the table in the shadows sat a figure. "Oh"—Constance was startled—"there you are . . . I thought I was alone."

"I'm speechless." The voice was Alfie's, she could see that now. "You look so beautiful."

She made a mock bow. "Thank you. Jerry, where are you? Am I early? Too early?"

"He's inside doing the donkey work," said Alfie. "He'll

be out in a minute. Sit down and talk to me. Sit close. Do you smell as good as you look?"

She held her wrist near Alfie's snub nose. "Arawak, do you like it?"

"Arawak? After the Indians? No French perfume that rocks the room?" She could have sworn Alfie's eyebrows went up.

"It's made in the Virgin Islands and I like it." She took cigarettes and lighter from her small bag. "I'm getting chauvinistic where the Caribbean is concerned." She raised her voice—silly, of course he could hear her anyway, he was talking to her through Alfie. "Jerry, can I help you with anything?" And almost jumped when his voice, just behind her, answered. "All done, thank you. Alfie, you're remiss. You haven't done the honors for Constance. Will you share some champagne with me or do you prefer something stronger?"

"Champagne? My goodness, a special occasion? Yes, thank you. I happen to like champagne very much. It's a throwback to all those movies in the nineteen thirties, all those glamorous women in backless dresses holding champagne glasses. Kay Francis and Mary Astor."

Jerry moved to the patio bar, asked over his shoulder, "You, too, Alfie?"

Constance joined the game. "Of course he will. Aren't we elegant, silver stand and all? Jerry, you do very well for a bachelor, all the ruffles and flourishes . . ." She stopped en route to the bar, looked into the dining area where a table was meticulously set for two. "Just you, just me, Jerry?" she asked.

Alfie's voice retorted. "Of course not! I'm your chap-

eron. Do you need a chaperon, Connie? On Anguilla you
were so proper—"

"And that will be enough out of you. Children should
be seen and not heard. Here you are, Connie, a bit of the
bubbly. Let's walk down to the beach, out of earshot of
this brash young man, where we'll sit under a chikee and
bay at the moon if we feel so inclined. I'll bring the wine
bucket if you'll take the glasses. Careful now, don't spill
on your beautiful dress. You do look lovely tonight, but
then you always look lovely."

Connie didn't ask the question until they were seated
beneath the chikee. "What's wrong, Jerry?"

He set the silver wine bucket on the sand between
them, and sipped from his glass. "You can tell? Of course.
But think how lucky I am, I can take it all out on Alfie
and nobody's feelings are hurt."

"It sounded to me as though Alfie was taking it out on
you."

"Alfie is inclined to do that, he's a fighter. You know
Alfie never takes an insult lying down. We have a slam
session, Alfie and I, and then we both feel better for it.
Let's forget the little dummy. Will you look at that moon?
So full it's about to spill over. I ordered it just for you."

Constance looked. "Are you courting me, Jerry?"

"Wooing is a much nicer word, don't you think? Alfie is
right in that respect, I do like the old words better. I wonder what they call it these days."

"I don't know. Making out? Perhaps the entire process
is a lost art. Wooing me—for what purpose, Jerry?"

"Here, let me refill your glass. My intentions, I assure
you, are strictly honorable."

She watched him carefully pour the liquid to the top of

her goblet. "I hate to spoil your dinner party, Jerry, but I don't think I'll ever remarry. If that's what you mean by having honorable intentions."

He smiled. His eyes were black, and the moonlight gave them silver glints. "Don't rush things, Connie. Wooing takes time, we'll talk about that later. Now we'll just enjoy, say nice things to each other and delicately probe."

"Delicately probe. For secrets? We should tell each other secrets?"

"Perhaps. Drink up, you're much too tense. You're acting like a teenager on her first date, as though you've never been alone with a man."

"It's been a long time."

"Nonsense. We were alone on Anguilla."

"That was different."

"How?"

"You were different. Then you were—just a companion. You could have been—anybody. You know what I mean."

"No. I don't. Explain."

She bit her lip. "You aren't probing delicately."

"Sometimes you have to puncture the surface before you can delicately probe."

She started to rise and dribbled champagne on her skirt. "Jerry, I don't want to be—reached."

"Here, use my handkerchief. Oh, I know you've built your own personal castle complete with drawbridge and turrets." He patted her hand. "Honestly, my dear, I'm not attacking. I'm humbly requesting permission to come in for a visit. After that, we'll see. What do you say? Is the queen in residence?"

His tone was so gentle, his expression so compassionate, she felt an absolute fool.

"Yes"—she held out her champagne glass—"the lady of the house is at home. But be advised, there are guards on the ramparts."

Alfie's voice responded, "And a monster in the moat."

A stray breeze blundered out of the stillness. Constance shivered slightly from its sudden chill. It was gone in seconds. Wavelets ran onto the sand without sound. "Jerry." Connie leaned forward to scratch an ankle. "I'm being eaten alive by sand fleas. Let's go in."

"I'm an only child. Do you have brothers and sisters, Connie?"

They'd eaten and were having brandies on the porch. The moon had moved across the island so that they sat in shadow, the only light being a pair of hurricane lamps gleaming softly.

"One younger sister," she said, leaning back on the chaise. She was completely relaxed; the food had been delicious, the wine excellent, and the conversation had been about other people. "She lives in Connecticut and considers St. Martin the end of the uncivilized earth. But, then, of course, she's never been here. She has a husband and college-age children. Her ambition is to move someday to Florida."

"I envy you. You have someone to leave your money to."

Constance raised her eyebrows. "That's a peculiar statement." She grinned wryly. "If that's why you're courting me, be advised that I don't have that much money."

He answered seriously, "Oh, I'm pretty sure that I have more than you as far as that goes. You've never had to think about the problem, but I have. I worked hard for what I have and by some standards I'm a fairly rich man. I'm also getting along in years, as they say, and the returns from investments keep rolling in so that it's clear to me I'll never be able to spend it all even if I turned into a raving extravagant. So—who do I leave it to? Or, as Alfie would say in his supercilious way, to whom do I leave it?"

"Good works? Deserving strangers? God knows there's plenty of need."

"True. All too true. But the years have turned me into a cynic, my dear. How do I find the truly good works, the deserving strangers? Furthermore, there's the biblical philosophy that money is the root of all evil. How do I know that I won't do more harm than good in giving? The Tosca private welfare foundation—take, for instance, the good people of this island. Some twenty thousand people on both sides? Let's pick a figure—an arbitrary figure. Say that ten thousand of them could use the money to good purpose. It would take a million dollars to give each a hundred dollars and what use is a hundred dollars? It won't send a child to school off-island, it won't build a house or add a bathroom or even buy a stove for the kitchen. All my hard-earned money would be frittered away and six months later they'd have forgotten that they ever had it."

"You have given it a great deal of thought, haven't you?" Constance found the subject slightly distasteful. "Set up a foundation, then, with someone reliable to run it."

He shook his head. "It takes the likes of Rockefeller or Ford money to set up a foundation—that much I haven't got."

"You mentioned school—build a school for the island, there's a need for more schooling."

"I don't think either government would like me sticking my foreign nose in their educational system."

Constance swallowed the last of her brandy; it was time to go home. "You know what I think? I think you're jumping the gun, feeling morbid. You've a great many years left to figure this all out. You're just feeling unloved and unwanted." This time she patted his hand. "Don't worry, Jerry, someone worthy will turn up." She thought, Isn't it too bad that you can't take it with you? Immediately she realized that that was unfair, and was glad that she hadn't said it.

"What do you think we've been talking about all eveing?" he asked softly.

Constance stood. "Sire, you can take your caskets of gold and diamonds or whatever they are right back where they came from! The drawbridge is shut and the queen is going home." At the edge of the porch, she stopped, said, "Thank you very much for a lovely dinner."

She stopped again at the top of the steps. "And thank you, I guess, for the lovely bribe."

Alfie answered from the shadows, "Don't be mad at him, Connie. All his life he's been a silly ass. If he didn't have me to look after him, God knows . . ."

She went on down the steps, and thought as she crossed to her car that she heard a conversation. Jerry's voice, then Alfie's, then Jerry's.

★   ★

People were arriving. Doria's dinners were always popular, but tonight seemed to be a gathering of the clans. I accepted a second drink from Allan. He seemed in a strange mood. He was talking a lot, in a loud voice—that wasn't like him—but then he had to be loud, the bar was crowded and still people were coming in.

Doria came to help Allan and the bartender. "I don't know where they all came from," she muttered. "I just hope the food holds out, half of them didn't make reservations."

"Can I help?"

She shook her head. "They're doing all they can in the kitchen. Well, for goodness' sakes! Fran Crawford, and Jack. How are you?"

"It must be something in the air," Allan said under

his breath. Someone jostled my elbow at that moment, causing my drink to spill, and as I gasped in annoyance, the lights went out.

The crowd groaned in chorus, as though they'd rehearsed it.

"Damn, damn, damn." Allan cursed the darkness and the electric company. Doria lit a candle in a hurricane holder, which enabled her to light others. "We'll never get dinner on the tables now," she complained sotto voce, carrying a candle kitchenward.

"Drinks on the house," announced Allan, so I had another one.

Someone who'd watched the time said it was nearly an hour before the electricity came back on. When it did I wasn't sure whether I cared about eating at all, but Doria appeared and shooed us all to tables so I went with Allan. I was just sitting there, waiting, staring at the candle flame when I heard a voice, I don't know whose, saying from somewhere behind me, "But I just saw Greg Brady this afternoon—what do you mean, he's disappeared?"

Everything leaked out through a hole in the floor into a big black pit, taking me with it.

A fuzzy face, floating over my head, asked, "When did you eat today? Did you eat at all?" I blinked. The face became Brett's.

"I fainted, didn't I? I knew I was about to, but I couldn't do anything about it." And then I remembered. "Greg. Someone said they saw Greg." I tried to sit up, I was lying on the sofa in Doria's private living room.

Brett frowned. "I don't know anything about that, we'd just come in and there you were, draped over the table." The "we," of course, included Morry Bunty who peered at me over Brett's shoulder.

"Susan?" Doria spoke from the doorway. "Are you all right? Is she all right, Brett?"

"I'm all right," I told her. I was, oddly enough; I felt very sober. "Doria, did you hear—who said they saw Greg?"

Doria looked blank. "Greg? Someone said they'd seen Greg?" She half-turned as though she'd go ask, then changed her mind and looked back again, her face troubled.

"We'll take care of her, Doria." Brett stretched out a hand to me. "Feel like getting up? Morry, get the lady some grub, I think she's on the verge of starvation."

★   ★

She'd lost it, lost it. What did she care about Susan Brady—she had Constance Cobble to worry about. Constance hadn't read it, but according to the New York *Times* list of best sellers, a recent one had had something to do with looking out for number one.

Days had passed—five of them—and Susan still lay on that couch at Doria's with everybody catering to her while she babbled on about Greg. Jerry hadn't come near since the dinner party, even Agnes was avoiding her, which was a blessing. Her only circled date on the calendar was tomorrow morning, 9:30 A.M. TV, Cleo James read the notation and that was a drag, whatever would they talk about. Maybe she could tell some droll little tales of the island . . . here was an incident, Felix, aged maybe thirteen or fourteen, merry-eyed, rides by on a donkey. He carries something in his hands, something she gets only a glimpse of. She asks, "Felix, what have you got there?"

Felix turns, holds out his treasure. "Turtle, see?" As turtles go, this one is probably a teenage turtle, perhaps even a contemporary of Felix—could they have been born on the same day? Felix beams. "You want to buy him?"

She laughs, shakes her head; it is somewhat of a pose, she wishes the turtle were back in the sea, but she likes Felix, wants to say something pleasant. "No, but I like your donkey." A lovely beast with eyelashes.

Felix grins broadly, teeth flashing, eyes ashine. "You want to buy him?"

When she was a little girl and her name had been Connie Fielding instead of Constance Cobble, she had announced her intention of writing mystery stories. Most of those who heard this announcement smiled indulgently, some even laughed, but a few frowned, including her mother. "Where in the world did she get such an idea?" she asked Connie's father.

"How should I know?" had been her father's reply and there was, indeed, no way to know because Connie didn't know herself. As ambitions go, it had been number four, starting with nursing, secretarial work and toe dancing. It was, nonetheless, the dream with staying power because here she was, all these years later, "the well-known mystery writer, Constance Cobble."

Had her mother been alive, Connie might have talked to her. "I'm having trouble with my writing and that's serious because I'm a writer, nothing else, and if I can't write, then what am I? I've learned all the rules, I've worked hard. What's happened?" And that would have been a waste of breath because her mother, even if she was alive, would have frowned in total incomprehension.

As would anyone she could think of. Even Roger. And yet because it was so very important, she had to talk it out with someone. She explained to Roger.

"I must get on with it. The money isn't so important, you left me enough if I'm careful, but if I can't do what I do best I can't do anything, don't you see?"

Constance lowered her voice. If anyone should be coming up the drive, they'd think she was . . . "I'm frightened, Roger. I'm terrified. It was a gift, after all, and I'm afraid I've wasted it like we've wasted water and fuel and trees . . ."

Get on with it, she told herself, stop whining and get on with it . . . get rid of the guilt by writing about other people's loves and hates and deadly impulses . . .

Scene: nine-thirty the next morning. Here is our heroine, dressed prettily, smiling nicely at Cleo James who is black and beautiful, smiling and telling lies: "Well, I've decided to write my life story. I almost said memoirs, but that's a pretentious word, don't you think?"

"I'd love to read it, Ms. Cobble." (Cleo James was up-to-date.) "Biographies and autobiographies are my favorite kind of reading. Have you thought of a title?"

Title? I haven't even thought of a plot! It should begin with Roger's death, then flash back. Because Roger's death was the grabber, actually the only important thing that had ever happened to her. But that was the climax, too, so if she led off with her climax, then she'd shot her

wad. . . . She was aware of a loud silence; she was, she
thought, supposed to say something and she hadn't been
listening. She looked ceilingward for help. There were
lights up there, dozens of them it seemed, all shining
down on her. "It's very warm in here." She smiled so Cleo
James would understand she wasn't complaining. "All
those lights." She pointed upward.

"Yes, that's one of the inconveniences we learn to put
up with. Sorry." A smile from Cleo, not a pleased one.
"How many books have you written?"

She was happy to have heard the question even if she
wasn't sure of the answer. "I'm not quite sure—forty-
some, I think. One loses track." Another smile for Ms.
James; this one meant, please don't think I'm being patronizing.

"Where do you get your plots?" Constance tried not to
wince and hoped she'd succeeded, but maybe not because
Cleo James went on, "I mean, do you do the end first or
the beginning?"

"The characters. The people are the story, you see. So I
start with them—in particular a protagonist, and that protagonist dictates the crime. Well, for instance, if it's a
woman then she'll commit a certain kind of crime for a
certain reason while if it's a man his crime and his motive
will be different, you see . . ."

She was perspiring and her voice sounded shaky, and
she caught a glimpse of herself on the monitor, awful!
Damn, damn, damn you, Horace . . . you got me into
this, it was interminable . . . oh, thank God, it was
ending.

"Thank you very much, Ms. Cobble, for joining me on
Channel Three this evening. I'm sure you've been an in-

spiration to the young people here on St. Martin who might like to write mystery novels."

The lights went off and the place, in contrast, seemed dark. People were moving around. Cleo James had moved away, she realized, but she couldn't seem to get up from her chair. There was something holding her; she stopped breathing to hear. A sound. Muffled. Surreptitious. Something, someone moved in the shadows, something meant her harm, something came closer.

"Are you all right, Mrs. Cobble?" Cleo James was bending over her.

She rose. "Yes, thank you. It was just—so warm. I hope I didn't ruin your show, Ms. James."

"Of course not. Not at all. May I help you to your car? Would you like a glass of water? I can get you one from the dressing room." Sleek Ms. James was fluttering around her like a tiny bird mother.

She told her again how fine she was and proved it by walking steadily to the doorway, out the door, across the parking lot, sliding into the car, shutting the door, starting the engine and driving off.

Get up. Susan Brady, get up, let's get on with it, why are you resisting me so? She pulled typing paper and carbon from her machine, crumpled it savagely and threw it across the room. "Temper, temper," said Jerry from the gallery from where he could look through the window.

Constance jumped and so he added, "Sorry. Didn't mean to frighten you."

"You didn't. I'm just in what people used to call a snit because of a noncooperative heroine." She went out to join him and they sat on the wicker chairs. "Where have you been? I thought you were sending anti-Constance signals by silence."

"I've been preparing for a TV spectacular." He grinned. "With Cleo James. You've no idea how out of practice Alfie is."

She grimaced. "I've already made a fool out of myself. Did you see it? I hope not."

"It wasn't that bad."

"It was positively, absolutely terrible. Yet there is a silver lining; Agnes told me the reception was so bad at her house they could hardly hear and couldn't see very well either. Maybe it was that bad all over the island. God, I hope so."

"You ain't seen nuthin' yet. What's that from, *Showboat*? At any rate, I've decided that Alfie and I have taken up the wrong profession. He should have been the ventriloquist and I should have been—well, I've always wanted to be a Harvest Moon Ball champion."

"You're kidding."

He shook his head. "For two years of my palmiest days I spent every Friday night at Roseland. Saturdays I went to Johnny Phillips' studio in the Bronx. Have you heard of Johnny Phillips? He was a great dance instructor."

"What kind of dancing did he instruct?"

"Ballroom, of course. You remember, when couples touched? Together they danced. According to a pattern. One-step, two-step, fox-trot, waltz. The Lindy. Conga, rhumba, samba, tango, mambo. And jitterbug. Jitterbug had a pattern, if you remember. A style."

She looked at him, surprised. "I'm a terrible dancer."

"What makes you think so? We'll try it sometime—maybe tonight. How would you like to go dancing tonight? With an almost Harvest Moon champion?"

"I couldn't." She gestured back toward the typewriter. "I promised myself I would stick at this until I finished my literary epic. Ask me again when the crisis is over—maybe next year." She patted his hand to let him know she wasn't entirely serious.

Jerry leaned back against the cobra back of his wicker

chair. "Did I ever tell you about my grandfather and the brass bed? He had a summer home on an island off Maine. He was a very positive man. Used to getting his own way. Well, there was only one plumber on his island, a Mr. Phiffelman. These two gentlemen were very formal with one another—it was Mr. Phiffelman and Mr. Tosca even though I've heard it said that Mr. Phiffelman considered Grandfather merely 'one of those summer people.'

"Well, Grandfather owned a very handsome brass bed which he sent up to the island house. He decided after a bit that the bed was too high—it had proved to be a chore climbing in and crawling out—so he instructed Mr. Phiffelman to cut off the ornate brass legs 'exactly six inches.'"

"Exactly six inches? All four legs?" She could anticipate the joke, two too short, two too long . . .

"Well, when Grandfather got back to the island he found the bed at exactly the height he'd designated and he was delighted. Until one morning when he dropped his collar button which promptly rolled under the bed. Grandfather tried to pull the bed out to retrieve the collar button but he couldn't budge the thing. It was then that he discovered Mr. Phiffelman's technique—he had simply drilled four holes in the floor, built little platforms and lowered the bed."

Constance laughed. "I don't believe you. Mr. Phiffelman, indeed!"

Jerry looked solemn and crossed his heart. "*C'est vrai.* Mr. Phiffelman was quoted as saying, 'Ain't that just like them summer people, fixing to ruin a perfectly good bed when they was such an easy way to fix it?' It took my grandfather ten years or more to see the humor but by the end of his life, he could smile at the story."

"Mr. Phiffelman exists in many places, not only in Maine."

"Ah, yes, Mr. Phiffelman is legion. He had some interesting solutions to plumbing problems. Better not tell Alexandre, our estimable plumber, but here's one: Grandfather, sitting in the parlor one day, looked out and said, 'It's raining.' Grandmother, on the other side of the room, looked out, said, 'No, the sun is shining.' Mr. Phiffelman had run the drain from an upstairs washbasin right out Grandfather's side of the building and my father was upstairs washing his hands."

Constance found herself becoming fond of Mr. Phiffelman. "Can I get you something? Coffee? Tea?"

"No, I'm going home because you look now as though you'd like to go back to your typewriter and Alfie can use some more practice for our upcoming performance. I'll come by for you about seven."

"All right. But no dancing."

"We'll see. I'll bring you some Ginger Rogers pills. And don't be so bossy. You might end up being an old maid."

And when he had gone she did feel better and Susan Brady did respond, she got up off that sofa and said, "I think I'd better go home, no, no, I'll be all right, thank you very much, no, I really couldn't eat a thing, yes, Doria, I'll call you . . ."

It wasn't much, perhaps, but it got her off that sofa and now Constance could go on.

Constance didn't go dancing after all because her editor was coming to St. Martin; a cable received that very afternoon had told her so. Arriving August 9, staying five days, ALM flight 292, that's what the cable had said. Why hadn't Vera put down the arrival time? Now she'd have to make a special trip to the airport to find out when ALM flight 292 got in. She could never remember flight arrival times; there were so many planes and they kept changing them around.

And why was Vera coming? Because she hadn't finished the book, that was why. All right, August 9, that was almost a week away, well, six days. She'd finish it. That was all, no interruptions, she'd finish it and then when Vera climbed down from the plane in her blue jeans —how could anyone her age have an attractive young editor who could have been her daughter if she'd had a daughter, who wore blue jeans and whose hair curled like morning glory vine? There was something very wrong when editors looked like fashion models.

Finish the book.

She hefted the box containing the carefully typed pages. The box felt heavy, as though the book was done. But that was because what was done was in triplicate; she had not finished with Susan and Susan had not finished with her.

She opened the box and began to read what she had written, which was always difficult. Because what she wanted to write and what she wrote were two different things. No *To Kill a Mockingbird* or *In Cold Blood* or *The Once and Future King* or *Gaudey Night* or *Murder in the Calais Coach* or . . .

★   ★

Antoine's studio-home was a three-room shingled shack, with a faded red corrugated zinc roof. A mauve bougainvillea clung to one corner. Antoine's flowers were pale but his paintings were not. He created great shouting views done in primary reds, yellows, blues, then combined these in exciting clean colors. The tourists loved them, they were forever emerging from the shuttered doors of Antoine's shack, brown-paper-wrapped parcels in hand. Original art, duty free. Many of them came then to my shop, Antoine's being across the way.

I owned some Antoine prints but none of his oils. For one thing, they were expensive and, for another, the ones I wanted always turned out to be the ones he wouldn't sell. They hung on the walls of his shack, turning it into a museum with blazing squares and oblongs of color hidden from outside eyes by pale shingled walls.

"Antoine. Ho—Antoine!"

I heard a faint response from the rear of the building. I followed the sound and found Antoine clad as usual in shorts forming a mosaic of broken glass, mostly green Heineken beer-bottle glass polished by the sea. "Red," he muttered, "I need red and blue." He glanced up, smiled. "Those colors are hard to come by. Blue, sometimes, I find."

"From a Bromo Seltzer bottle," I suggested, but he didn't know what a Bromo Seltzer bottle was, I could tell. "Antoine, at Doria's last night, did you hear someone say they'd seen Greg?"

Antoine didn't look up from his mosaic. He was trying to fit a white piece into an odd-sized hole. "I wasn't at Doria's last night, Susan."

I looked at him as though he'd gone crazy. Maybe he had. I knew I'd seen him coming in just after the lights came on before I fainted. He would have been in a perfect position to hear whoever it was who said . . . "You weren't there?" I said stupidly.

Now he looked up. "No." He frowned. "You saw me? You think you saw me there?"

I nodded.

Antoine gazed at some faraway thing. "That's interesting. I was here, working. But I was thinking about you and Greg at one time. Perhaps we made some connection." He was looking at me with interest. "Perhaps we can do that again. Set up an experiment. Are you interested?"

I nodded numbly. I wasn't interested at all, I was
terrified. I had seen him. He was lying. Why was he
lying? Did Antoine know something about Pauline's
murder, about Greg's disappearance? Did he know
something he wouldn't tell? Oh, I thought, how dangerous, and I said it aloud, "If you know something
about Greg—or Pauline—you should tell me, Antoine.
Tell somebody. It's dangerous to know something
and not tell anyone. All the books show how dangerous . . ."

He was smiling gently, but there was no smile in
his eyes. "When I was thinking of you last night I
was thinking that this is all very hard for you. I
would like to help you, I really would. We could
hold a meeting, at a special time, at a special place,
in the hills, I think. Signs and omens live more com-
fortably in the hills where there are no untoward
sounds to disturb them."

Something inside writhed and I realized it was
fear. Meetings in the hills . . . "I don't think—I don't
believe in obeah or jumbies."

This time his smile was patronizing. "Oh, I'm not
into obeah, I'm into pyramids. Do you know that if
you build yourself a pyramid-shaped room . . ."

I backed away. "Tell me later, Antoine," I said, "I
think I've got a customer." I had no customer this
quiet off-season day, and come to think of that, I
didn't want a customer. So I shut the doors to the
shop and locked them and sat in the back listening to
the sound of the sea with my eyes stretched wide because when I closed them I saw Pauline Gray's hair

floating, curling, a strange new brand of sea anemone.

And I thought, isn't it strange, I didn't realize I had grown to hate Greg until I'd lived without him.

It had grown quite dark when I heard the phone ringing. Did I want to answer it? I didn't know. It rang again and again. Make a bargain with the telephone: if it rings ten times, then answer it. Because if it rings ten times that means that whoever is on the other end really wants to talk to me . . . five, six, would he give up, seven, eight . . . two to go . . . nine, ten, ah, but I had to go inside and that would take time, surely he would hang up before I got there so don't bother . . . no sir, you promised, you made a bargain . . . "Hello?"

"Susan." The voice was very faint, it sounded like a sighing breeze. "Susan."

"Who—who is this?"

"Help me. It's dark. And damp and cold. Come get me, Susan. Bring me back."

I swallowed but not enough to get rid of the blockage in my throat so I swallowed again. "Who is this?" My voice was shrill. Someone was playing a nasty game. "Who *is* this?"

"Oh, Susan." So soft, so sad. "I'm going to hang up," I told the telephone, "and I shan't answer again so don't bother to ring. In the morning I shall go to the gendarmes and then we will go to the telephone company and then we shall catch you, my friend . . . do you hear me? You'll get into trouble for this."

"Susan . . ." I hung up and found that tears were running down my cheeks. I went to the kitchen and turned on the light. Two cockroaches scurried into cracks. I poured gin into a glass and tried to drink it straight but couldn't get it down, had to mix tonic with it and ice. After I'd had enough of them, sitting in the darkness with the sound of the sea, I became ready to sleep and dragged myself up the stairs, fell into bed, alone, no one to hear me, no one to help me up.

There are two shuttered windows and a shuttered door leading off my bedroom—our bedroom. Already I am beginning to refer to things as mine rather than ours, and there you can add a scale or two to my guilt pack. I slept with the shutters wide open. Usually I loved the instant decor: black velvet with diamonds, otherwise known as sky and stars. Come, come, Susan, that's arch and trite. Damn all those people who said, sang or wrote such phrases over and over again—why couldn't I have been the first?

One moment I was buried alive and the next I was wide-awake with the certain knowledge that someone was in that room with me. My heart jumped up and kicked me. To add to that pain I banged my head on a shutter so quickly did I sit up in bed. "Who's there?" I was proud of my voice, it was not shaky. I was tough, wasn't I?

"I've come to take you to your husband," said Morry Bunty.

I stopped rubbing my head. "Where? Where is he?" Now my voice shook.

"You don't ask if he's all right."

"Is he all right?" I didn't ask if he was all right! The nerve. Creeps into my house, my bedroom, announces he's taking me to Greg and then complains that I don't ask the right questions.

"I'd say he's felt better and he's felt worse. You'll see soon. I'll wait in the other room while you get dressed."

Wait, I've got it now, I'm dreaming; it must be a nightmare. Yes, that's it. All right, let's get this straight. Start from Pauline Gray. We find Pauline Gray. Greg begins to act funny and then he disappears and nobody says it to my face but everybody believes that Greg killed Pauline and then got off the island somehow, and all these things are facts. So why is someone trying to scare me to death?

That was it—they weren't! I was dreaming that, too. I was beginning to think there was something wrong with me but now that I've realized I was dreaming . . .

"Are you ready? We don't have all night." I couldn't seem to wake up. Morry's voice came from the living room. His face, a pale balloon, floated in the doorway.

"I'm not going. I'm not going with you." It was time for the dream to change, for Morry Bunty to dissolve.

The pale balloon hung in the darkness above my bed. "You mustn't keep him waiting any longer." His voice sounded eerie, not really like Morry's voice—if I wasn't dreaming, then maybe he was drunk. That must be it. What did he want? Not money. Me? Surely not. He wasn't the type, I wasn't the type.

I slid my legs over the side of the bed and stood up. "Go in the living room while I put some clothes on." Truly awake now, I was curious. Perhaps he was serious, he had really found Greg. Was that possible? In the night many unlikely things seem possible.

He drove Brett's car very fast. There was no other traffic as we sped through Orleans, past Belle Plaine, crossing the French-Dutch border. He was silent too, and we rode like two ghosts through the star-filled night.

The road to Brett's castle went round the mountain like striations on a top. I couldn't see the house or the top of the mountain and yet suddenly we were there, stopped before the iron gates faintly lit from somewhere inside. I'd thought the house would be ablaze with light but no, barely more than moonlight, artificial—the light from a television set? Of course, directly inside the entrance someone watched television.

Greg? Greg watching television in a castle atop a mountain? I *was* dreaming.

"Get out," Morry ordered.

I pushed at the door catch so that it opened. "Aren't you coming? Where's Brett?"

"Come in, Susan luv." Brett stood beside the huge ceramic boxer dog next to the doorway. He blocked even more of the light so that he and the dog were faceless in the shadow.

I got out of the car. "Morry said—he frightened me, Brett. He said Greg was here. I couldn't believe— If he is here, it can only mean bad news."

"Oh, he's here all right."

I began to cry. "I want him to be gone, I want him to get away with it. She was an evil woman, she tempted him, she taunted him until he had to kill her. That's how it happened, I know."

"Did he tell you that?"

"No." Morry still sat in the driver's seat, I stood beside the car, Brett and the dog were statues in the doorway. "He was ashamed, he couldn't tell me but I know him so well." I stepped closer so that I could see his face. He stepped backward at the same moment and I could see the red eyes of the dog as we danced our little pas de deux. "Aren't we going inside?"

He let me pass. The television set held no picture, just light flashing eternally across a black screen. "You forgot to turn it off," I said.

"He likes it." Morry spoke from just behind me. I all but jumped.

"It's a most flattering light for an aging actor whose last face-lift is slipping." Brett spoke for himself.

"Where is he?" I asked abruptly. Enough of this verbal Ping-Pong.

"Ah." Brett contemplated the far end of the room. Pictured in its vast areas of glass was the black sky studded with stars, but over here, hanging outside Brett's mountain, it didn't seem so friendly.

"Come with me," Brett urged, and Morry gave me a push—more like a small shove.

"Where?" They didn't answer, but simply moved away, so I went with them. Outside the living room, I saw the stars and moon reflected in the swimming pool, walked along the catwalk that clung to the mountain, turned toward one of the guest suites, and

ended up at a large structure with crenellated parapet. It was, I knew, the cisterns for Brett's castle, the
source of water up here. They were, I'd been told,
the largest cisterns on the island—large enough to
supply a village. But then one couldn't pipe desali-
nated water up the mountain (one could but it would
cost one an arm and a leg), and one had difficulty
persuading the lumbering water trucks to bring it up.

Brett had produced a flashlight which shone now
on steps leading up to the top of the battlements. I'd
been frightened from the first whisper from Morry;
now I was getting panicky. "What are you doing?
Why should I go up there? Stop pushing, I won't go,
I won't—stop it!"

Thanks to Morry I stumbled up the steps hard on
Brett's heels. Once there, Brett took a fast hold of
one arm and shoulder, and pressed me forward.
Guided by the flashlight, Morry bent to raise the
trapdoor that permitted me to look into the cistern. I
raised my eyes to the stars. "Don't," I said, "don't."

No one answered for a moment, then, "Look." My
arm was twisted. "There. Look."

"No." I wouldn't. I couldn't.

Hands turned my head. I closed my eyes.

"See how he looks up at you, Susan. See how
peacefully your husband floats. Look." Brett's voice
was hard, his grasp harder.

"No," I cried, "no!"

"Look," he said, "or I'll throw you in with him."

I looked. And passed out. They caught me, kept
me from falling in with that dreadful bloated thing,
and carried me back to the house. I came to on a sofa

in the living room where the television still gleamed.

"What are you going to do?" I asked the two men who sat looking at me.

Brett shrugged. "Leave him there. The water in that cistern is contaminated, of course, but we can use it for the gardens. Morry and I thought first of calling the police but we decided against it. For one thing, they might not believe we didn't put him there."

"Yes," I agreed. "They well might think you had. Especially if I told them about my suspicions."

"You would do that, wouldn't you?" Brett smiled his charming smile. "That's why we decided to help you leave the island. That's what you want to do, isn't it?"

"Yes, but it's impossible. Maybe eventually. For one thing, I have to sell the business—it's my only source of income since I can't collect his insurance until everyone's convinced he's dead."

"I'll buy you out. Morry, where's the paper? Here, we've drawn up an agreement. All we have to fill in is the amount."

I sat up. "Well, it's worth—at least fifty thousand, I'd say. It's hard to know without an up-to-date inventory." They looked weird in the eerie light. Again I had that funny feeling I was dreaming.

"I'll give you a hundred thousand." Brett spoke so casually he might have said a hundred dollars instead of a hundred thousand. "That suit you?"

"Yes. Yes. I think so."

"Write the amount in, Morry. Done? Okay, Susan. Sign right there. We'll sign after."

"I can't read it in this light."

"We'll fix that." He switched on the flashlight, then he shone it on the papers. It was straightforward enough: it declared that Brett Carlisle agreed to pay Susan Brady the sum of one hundred thousand dollars for her shop on St. Martin, for the inventory, the furnishings, and all accoutrements. I signed the original and carbons. It was a windfall beyond my expectations.

Brett signed, then told Morry to witness. Brett kept the original and handed me the carbon. "And now"—flashlight off, he sat back in his chair, partially hiding his eyes with his hand—"tell us how you did it."

"I thought you'd want to know why."

"Oh, I know why. Pauline told me all about it—she spent a good many nights up here."

I leaned forward, "She was evil, you know. A beautiful woman, the most beautiful I've ever known, but evil. I started out being jealous of her, then I realized she didn't want my husband, she wanted me. You can imagine—no you can't—the agony I went through. I was attracted, all right, more than attracted. I didn't think Greg suspected a thing. I had legitimate errands that permitted me to be with her, but we'd been married a long time and I guess one can sense—changes. Anyway, after that smarmy jewelry salesman told the gendarmes he'd left a sample chain with us, I knew Greg was suspicious. I'd tried, up until then, to put the blame on him without being obvious, but day after day I saw him looking at me in a peculiar way and I knew he was thinking that I'd been away from the shop the day she died and that I'd denied seeing the chain when he knew perfectly well that I'd taken it for myself."

"He knew you killed her?" Morry, his eel eyes gleaming in the shadows, spoke. "That's pretty flimsy evidence."

"Well, I made a mistake there. I thought he knew but it turned out he was only puzzled. If I'd known that and thought up a good excuse, I wouldn't have had to kill him. But when he started to ask, I just assumed he knew so I blurted it all out and afterwards there was nothing else I could do. He might have been my husband, but he wouldn't have been that loyal. Still, I guess it's just as well, especially the way it's turning out. I couldn't live with him anymore and now I don't have to share the money."

Somebody sighed, I didn't know which of them. I shrugged. "Okay, so think I'm cold-blooded. Maybe I am."

Brett spoke softly. "When we found his body, we had a hard time figuring out how you did it physically. Dragging the body up on the parapet, that took some doing. What we didn't realize was how strong you are. You're a deceiving lady, Susan."

"Yes"—I was proud of that—"I am strong. And he wasn't a big man. He was unconscious, of course. I'd poisoned him at dinner. By the middle of the night he was in pain. I said I'd drive him to the doctor but instead I headed for your place. I knew she'd been seeing you and I thought what sweet revenge—if I'd known she'd been telling you about me!"

"You poisoned him? With what?"

"Rat poison. You just mix it with food. You've got to use a large dose for a man, of course. I stuffed an eggplant with a package mixed into the stuffing. It can't have much taste because he ate it with relish. Poor Greg. He always was a fool about Italian food and I fixed eggplant parmigiana." I studied the two of them. "What I can't understand is why you should help me."

Brett straightened up and smiled. "Why, Susan, you know you're one of our favorite playmates. And maybe I had my own reasons for being, maybe not pleased, but certainly not displeased to be rid of Pauline Gray. She had, shall we say, certain tendencies toward blackmail of one sort or another. How do you suppose she got her house? Just ask Mart Haven how much land he bought when he started to build and how much land he ended up with—but that's another story."

"You're getting the shop. It's a very good business, going to be better. You're not making a mistake there."

Another smile. "Yes, perhaps I've been longing to be a shopkeeper. It does get boring doing nothing, doesn't it, Morry?"

I still wasn't quite sure until I remembered, "But most of all, you're making sure you're above suspicion, aren't you? Buying me off gets rid of the Bradys once and for all and it will be thought that Greg killed Pauline and I helped him get away, then ran off to join him. That's what they'll think, isn't it? And that you took pity on me. You'll come out looking noble."

"Yes, indeed." Brett stood, stretched. "Well, it's time to be going. We've got a lot of ocean to cover before dawn."

"Ocean? Where are we going?"

"We thought we'd take you back to St. Kitts in the Bertram and leave you there. Get the bag, Morry. Morry collected a few clothes and your papers while he was waiting for you. I've added some cash, enough to keep you till we set up a bank account with the hundred thousand. A numbered account, maybe? In Curaçao, that might be a good idea. Yes, you write us as soon as you get there and we'll deposit the check to your numbered account and you'll be safe as houses."

"I might go on down to South America. Venezuela's right next door to Curaçao."

"Here's your bag. Are we ready? Let's get cracking then." He turned off the television set.

Somewhere in the middle of the Atlantic Ocean, maybe two hours later, Brett announced that he and Morry had enjoyed their part in my story, primarily because life had been so damned dull before. "And now, Susan, we've reached the end of the tale. We're going to pitch you overboard bag and baggage."

I laughed. "That's one easy way to save a hundred thousand dollars." Brett had a strange sense of humor but he had to make up for Morry who had no sense of humor at all.

"You're so right." Brett grinned. Something splashed in the water.

"Your bag," explained Morry. "Now you."

The old feeling—I was dreaming. None of this was

true, I had been dreaming, dreaming that Brett would leave me to die by drowning because no matter how good a swimmer one was eventually he would tire, or maybe before he tired, well, there were sharks out here in mid ocean. I was dreaming . . .

Turned out, I wasn't.

★ ★

The Rotary Club of St. Martin was sponsoring a beach picnic and Jerry had gotten tickets to the thing, which meant Constance had to go. Not that she minded going— she enjoyed the beach and picnics and the members who were, after all, island residents. It was the influx of tourists that she minded. They asked so many questions, so many of the same questions. She didn't enjoy being a walking talking autobiography. When she told that to Agnes once, Agnes had said (typical), "But they're very interested in you."

Sighed Constance, "Maybe, but I'm not very interested in me."

She surveyed her collection of swim wear, all rather elderly, before deciding she owed it to Jerry to invest in a new swimsuit and cover-up. At Pierre Lapin in Grand Case, Margaret Hodge, salesgirl extraordinaire, talked her into a Danskin against her doubts that it could control what could euphemistically be called a mature figure. Amazingly enough the surplice-fronted suit did all sorts of nice things in addition to its major delight—it felt as though she were wearing nothing. She found a bright, somewhat transparent pink and navy caftan to go over the navy blue suit and discovered she was quite pleased with her new outfit. I've a new image, she thought, sans whalebone avec see-through. Semi-demimonde. The concept amused her and she found herself smiling most of the drive home.

She found Jerry waiting on the gallery. "I wish you'd get a phone," he complained mildly. "I started to write a note but while rummaging for a pen I found your manuscript. I couldn't help reading—am I forgiven for that cardinal sin?"

"Yes, of course," she lied. "If you had written the note, what would it have said?"

"It would have said that we shall be three at the picnic, much to my regret. No, I don't mean that. I'm happy he's here. An old business associate has descended upon us and since he leaves Monday, I had to offer to share Sunday."

"Who is he?"

"My manager. Ex-manager, I should say. Barney Gingle. He's New York-born and -bred, if you know what I mean. I hope you don't mind."

She was amused. "I'm New York-born and -bred."

In Alfie's voice, he murmured, "Touché," mispronouncing it to sound like ouch. Constance laughed.

"But I don't mind, Jerry. It isn't as though he were interrupting a tête-à-tête."

"Oh? But I was hoping he was."

"With all those tourists baking on the sand? Run along with you now, I've work to do. If you read the ending, you know the book needs polishing."

"Some ending."

"Someday I'm going to write a book that ends like this: Blank space was the killer, of course. Then the reader can fill in blank space. Would they all be different, these write-in murderers? Or would they all be the same?"

"I would say that would depend on the writer."

"Yes, wouldn't it? I wonder which denotes more skill, an uncertain *neither black nor white* or a clear and concise *X marks the plot?*"

"I take it this is an up day. You tend to sparkle, my dear."

"Do I? That's nice. I wasn't sure I was up to that—another bad pun, forgive me. I'm always a little silly when a book's nearly done."

He kissed her cheek. "Stay that way. Barney and I will pick you up at nine-thirty tomorrow."

"Where's your friend staying?" It was a game she sometimes played, predicting character from the choice of hotel. There were, it seemed, La Samana people, the Mullet crowd, Caravanserai types, Pasanggrahan sorts. . . .

"The Beau Séjour," Jerry answered.

"Really?" It was a small, quiet French hotel, rather a surprising choice if Jerry's description was accurate.

"It was the only place he could get in. See you tomorrow, Connie. And be prepared."

"Prepared? For what?"

"You'll find out." A grin and he was gone down the

steps. She was smiling once more; he really was a dear man. "Do you like him, Roger?" she said aloud but didn't wait for an answer.

The Rotary beach party looked, from the upper deck of the Maison Maru, and then from the sea, like one of those Haitian paintings of a beach scene: sand was thickly speckled with stick figures while heads dotted the turquoise water. As the catamaran drew nearer, faces became identifiable.

Barney Gingle in person had been something of a surprise. He looked a great deal like Brett Carlisle who was, after all, totally imaginary and should not have a living counterpart. Just as Bootsie Baker should not have anything in common with Pauline Gray, not even manner of dying. Did it have to do with age, Constance wondered, this narrowing of the fine line between fact and fiction? At any rate, Barney Gingle, who should have resembled Morry Bunty, was another Brett and that had thrown her off; it required getting used to. Wouldn't it be nice to populate one's world with the sort of people one wrote about? Or would it? Would they get out of hand just as real people did and—yes, even so—book characters did as well?

"Connie? Come back from wherever. We've arrived." Jerry held out his hand to help her up. A steel band played on the beach, Barney was smiling, the sun was bright, a beautiful, beautiful day.

"I'm sorry." She smiled back at them. "I was novel-plotting, I'm afraid."

On the shore, beneath an umbrella, she watched Jerry stand in line for drinks at the makeshift bar where Len

Stein and Rein Heere played bartenders. He had a sweet face, really. He meant to ask her again to marry him, she knew that. Could she live with another person now? That was the unanswerable question. Never know until you try, alas . . .

". . . have you lived here, Connie?" Barney Gingle was speaking to her. The words she'd lost must have been "How long." She looked alert as though she'd been paying attention.

"Let me think, must be seven now. Yes, seven years." She waited for the next question.

It came. "Do you like it?"

"Yes, very much."

"There are quite a few Americans here?"

"Yes. Many more who have vacation homes and are here only part of the year."

"Some in business, too, I gather. I met a guy at the airport, odd sort of character, said he owned a restaurant and guest house around here somewhere. Named Cadwallader."

"Here you are, Connie, Bloody Mary as promised." Jerry was back with the drinks. Someone further down the beach had brought a guitar, was plunking away in counterpoint to the steel band, and, oddly enough, it didn't sound disharmonious.

"I'm wooing this lady, Barney." Jerry twinkled at her over the top of the Bloody Mary glass. "She said no but I won't accept that. Maybe today I'll catch her in a weak moment."

"Better take him on, Connie." She thought she caught an undertone of something less than enthusiasm in Gingle's voice but maybe it was only the bass of the guitar. "He's loaded, you know. Got nobody to spend it on."

"That's exactly the kind of remark that causes me to say no," she told them, smiling as she did so. Keeping it light.

"Aha!" Jerry gestured with his glass, spilling a little. "That does it. Tell her the truth, Barney, that I made a mint and threw it away, that I'm not only as poor as Job's turkey, I'm as poor as Job's goat. Why didn't you let me know sooner, Connie? I'd have taken immediate vows of poverty. Now will you marry me?"

Both of them were watching her, and she felt her face flush. "I'll think about it."

"Hurray!" This time Jerry spilled most of his drink, which made them laugh. He looked like a small boy when he went for refills. Gingle said, "We've been together a long time, Jerry and I. I guess you could say we're like brothers, two of a kind sometimes—other times, well, you know how it is. Strangers, almost. But he's a rare one. I guess you see that."

"I do. It's only that—well, I'm a widow who finds she rather likes living alone. I'm not sure at my age I could adjust to a new man, new habits . . ."

"At your age!"

"All right. Maybe I'm not old, but I'm not young."

"Younger than Jerry. Glad to see he picked someone near his age. When a guy's been a bachelor as long as he has, he sometimes chooses the wrong playmate."

"I take it you'd consider me the right playmate. Thanks, I think, for the compliment. Why didn't he? Ever marry, I mean."

Gingle shrugged. "I don't really know. That's one of

the bits we never talked about. I wouldn't ask and he wouldn't say. He had a widowed mother to support for a good many years. Matter of fact, she only passed on a couple of years back—that's when he came here. I guess she could be described as demanding in some ways. He was on the road a lot. He's a real worker, too—he had to be to get where he was. So maybe he never had time."

"And there's Alfie."

"Yeah." Double-take. "Alfie?"

"For company. He often talks to him."

Gingle grinned sheepishly. "It's the ventriloquist syndrome. After a while they can't help thinking the dummy is a little bit human. Don't hold it against him."

"Oh, I don't. I think it's rather charming." Better than talking to dead people, wasn't it?

"Hey, I like that song that guy's playing." Jerry was back with new drinks. "It's my philosophy, do you know it?" He hummed along with the guitar player, began to sing under his breath, "You got to know when to hold, know when to fold up, know when to walk away, know when to run. You never count your money when you're sitting at the table, there'll be time enough to count it when the dealing's done . . ."

"I'm for the steel band." Barney Gingle hummed, too, and "don't know the reason I stay here all season, nothing is sure but this brand new tattoo."

Jerry joined in, "But it's a real beauty, a Mexican cutie, how it got there I haven't a clue." And in harmony, "Wasting away again in Margaritaville, searching for my lost shaker of salt, some people claim there's a woman to blame, but I know it's my own damn fault. There's booze in the blender and soon it will render that frozen concoction that makes me hang on. . . ." Other people were listening, coming closer, the guitarist got to his feet, was playing now with the steel band and everything sounded good and everyone looked happy and the sun shone making a day of gold. Why not, thought Constance, why not marry him? Why not?

Agnes had been utterly ridiculous. Constance was sorry she'd asked her to act as her attendant but she'd been unable to think of anyone else who was close enough—not that she was that close to Agnes. But the foolish, girlish way she was going on about something old, new and blue set Constance's teeth on edge so she snapped at her.

Agnes, to Constance's amazement, burst into tears. "You wouldn't have talked to Bootsie Baker that way. The only reason you asked me was because she's dead."

"I would not have asked Bootsie Baker," she all but shouted. "I couldn't stand Bootsie Baker but now that I think of it she would have been preferable."

Agnes fumbled for a Kleenex in her copious tote bag. "You're not a very nice woman, Constance Cobble, not very nice at all." And suddenly this fat, wet-eyed woman had dignity. "Now I know why some people say you're a terror. I never believed them, but now I know."

"I'm sorry, Agnes. I do apologize, please forgive me. My nerves are on edge, if I've been a witch I didn't mean it." Oh, look at that pink rabbity nose twitch, Agnes did bring out the worst in her. She knew she had to control herself.

"Well . . ." A final wipe with the Kleenex. "I understand, I guess. It's not every day a girl our age gets married. As I was saying, I wonder if it's possible to dye flowers blue. If only we had some forget-me-nots, don't you think that would be so appropriate? But I don't suppose we could get any even from the States, I think it's the wrong time of the year . . ."

And Jerry was almost as bad. He fussed and fumed until she agreed and did, in fact, meet with lawyer John Carney from the States (down on vacation at his house in Grand Case, so convenient) to sign joint wills each leaving his worldly possessions to the other. Lawyer Ray Cromer, also on vacation at his house in Grand Case, was one witness and the French consul general another, so they could be pretty sure all loose ends were tied up in French and English.

They were married at the Mairie in Marigot. The civil service sufficed, they agreed, neither being church-affiliated. Agnes sniffled into the Saba lace handkerchief Constance had given her.

Barney Gingle couldn't stay for the wedding, so Jerry had to ask someone else to stand up for him. He wanted to ask Marty Lynn, he told Constance, but she said she didn't even know Marty Lynn. He was an artist in Grand Case, Jerry told her. "But I don't *know* him," she complained. So Jerry asked Horace Albertson who she really didn't like very much but at least was familiar. Horace wore a fancy ruffled shirt with drawstring pants and sandals. Agnes was all done up in a lacy caftan from Mexico that made her look like a frosted Volkswagen beetle.

The bride wore beige—oyster white, to be precise—an eggshell cone of gauze with vertical crocheted panels. The salesgirl had described it as simple but elegant. The groom, in white pants and navy blazer, might have stepped off his yacht. A pretty picture we make, thought Constance wryly. So different from that other wedding, another place, another time, another groom . . .

She hadn't dared to look at him even out of the corners of her eyes. He was so beautiful, so wonderful, she wondered how this miracle had come about. That she would be Mrs. Roger Cobble, that she would live in that fabulous house on Long Island, that she was the beloved of this charming, witty, wealthy man was almost more than she could believe. But it *was* true, here she stood at his side, now he would turn and lift the veil to kiss her, now . . .

"Connie." Jerry's voice brought her back. He leaned forward to kiss her, and she let him. It was over. They were man and wife.

Horace was giving the reception at his hilltop house, the very house Constance had used for Brett's residence. As she stood in the receiving line she could see the parapets of the fortlike cistern where she had had Susan drown Greg. It was a remarkable house with its huge patio encircling the swimming pool. More dramatic than the Cobble house on Long Island, but in the eyes of young Constance nothing had ever been more beautiful than that brick mansion with its white pillars and fan window above the wide white door. The gleaming brass door knocker was shaped like a stirrup, which was very fitting because there had been two riding horses in the small stable. What more could a woman want than a handsome husband and a beautiful home?

Well, for one thing, one could wish one hadn't found a husband of less than a day making drunken love to a member of the wedding party.

Not the matron of honor. The best man. Roger, it seemed, didn't care which sex was available. It took over six months for him to make the grade with the matron of honor. She had principles.

"E.B., how nice to see you. Jerry, this is Ebie Walker and right behind her are Norma and Lee Scott, Mary Scott, too." The line was a long one; Horace must have invited everyone on the island. Jerry knew many but not all of the guests. Constance prayed that she wouldn't experience an embarrassing name block. She relaxed her face a little, the smile was beginning to hurt.

A steel band was beginning to play, Horace hadn't left anything out.

"Jerry, here are Bill and Janet Hitchcock and Bill's sister, Louise Arnold. Anita! How nice to see you and Clemencia. Webb White you know, and Gordon and Marion Bent." She heard her voice sounding warm and sincere. She supposed she was sincere; these people in some degree or another were her friends and this was a very big day in her life. She should be happy.

She *should* be.

Why, then, did she have this undefinable, indescribable feeling of—feeling of—what? Gloom? Doom? Keep smiling, here was Roland Richardson, the artist. She'd borrowed a little bit of his personality for Antoine. "Ro, you know Jerry, don't you? Jerry owns one of your batiks, Ro. The one of the Goetz House."

Roland smiled at Jerry but kept hold of her hand. "Are you feeling all right, Constance?" he asked.

"Yes. Of course. Certainly. I feel fine."

He looked into her eyes a moment, then slowly nodded. "I'm happy for you," he said. "I wish you the best." He pressed her hand softly, "The very best." She hardly heard Gladys and Harold Crozier as they took Roland's place. She heard instead an echo from somewhere, nowhere. *You'll need it, you'll need it, you'll need it.*

Constance, driving Vera from the airport, listened to a monologue. "I'm not at all sure about Susan's part in all this," she said, referring to the book. "I liked her very much in the beginning, but less and less as the book progresses. Perhaps you need more emphasis on Greg's treatment of her. Show how his neglect brought out the latent lesbianism. But, of course, without tipping your hand." Constance looked thoughtful; at least that was her intent.

"I thought I made that clear enough," Constance told her. "I didn't want to hit the reader over the head with it."

"Oh, you didn't. You handled that— Oh, I see what you mean. Well, perhaps, but . . ."

"Vera, if you don't like the book just tell me." She slowed down for one of the "sleeping policemen," road bumps at Mullet Bay.

"But I *do*. Yes, on the whole I like it. I was just wondering—what would happen if Greg were rescued? By Morry, perhaps when he hears Susan's car that night. Instead of going back to sleep he gets up."

"But then he would see Susan. It took time to drag Greg up there and push him in." She didn't want Greg rescued. She wanted him dead.

"Well, maybe he could go up later for some reason—perhaps something went wrong with the water in the house and Brett sent him up to check the cistern, something like that?"

Constance held on tight to the steering wheel, they were riding over rough road now that they were out of the Mullet hotel complex. "It would be too late, he'd have drowned."

"Well, maybe not. I looked into it. There's something called a diving reflex in which oxygen is conserved for the heart and brain. It seems that some parts of the body such as arms and legs can go without oxygen for up to an hour. That's why you're not supposed to give up on resuscitation."

Constance shook her head. "Too technical. And besides, that makes it another story entirely."

"Well, yes. I guess it would. Fascinating though he is, I thought Brett a bit of a natural villain."

"Indeed he is. He and Morry murder Susan at the end just because it suits his sense of justice, in short, simply because he wants to. In my opinion, he is a true murderer. And worse than that, if there is a worse, he owns people. Such as Morry. I wonder what Morry did that enabled Brett to use him so. Killed his wife, more than likely."

Now that the car had reached pavement, Constance shifted into third and they picked up speed. She could feel Vera looking at her. "If you don't like the book, I'm sorry. I saw it that way."

"The book will be all right, Constance. Just a bit of rewrite here and there. It's you I'm concerned about. Concerned enough that I took time off to come down here for a few days. Only"—she laughed, it sounded like a put-on laugh—"to find that you've gone and got yourself married. Probably you don't need me at all."

"Why did you think I needed you?" There was an implication there that she didn't like. An implication that there was something wrong with Constance Cobble. Sorry, Constance Tosca. Would she ever get used to that?

Vera sensed her irritation. "I didn't think you needed me exactly—I mean, why would you need me, you have a sister, you have lots of friends, it was just that your recent letters have sounded so . . ."

"So—what?"

An exaggerated shrug. "Oh, I don't know. Bitter? No, that's not the word exactly. More like—aggressive." Again the sidelong glance.

Now Constance laughed. "As you can see, I'm anything but aggressive. Meek and mild Constance, that's me. I must have written off all my frustrations." She patted Vera's nearest hand. "For whatever reason, I'm glad to see you."

Vera sighed. "The things an editor is forced to do: come to this smiling, sunny island, lie beside the turquoise sea—I am going to lie beside the turquoise sea, am I not?"

"You surely are. As soon as we can manage it. Here's

home—Jerry and Alfie moved in with me, the house he was living in was rented so it would have been foolish for me to move there. And there they are waiting for us on the gallery. You can tell which one is the dummy, can't you, Vera?"

Vera caught Constance's arm as she started to get out of the car. "You are happy, aren't you, Constance?"

"Vera, what a question. I haven't been asked that since my salad days."

"I know, it's naïve. But I mean—you know what I mean. Is it all right? This marriage? Are you pleased that you married him?"

Constance tried to think of a suitable quip but none came to mind. "I don't know yet, Vera. It's only been a couple of weeks and it's just too soon to tell. Hi, Jerry— here's my Vera. Forgive her if she gives you short shrift, she's dying to get to the beach."

Driving Vera back to the airport, Constance realized she was sorry to see her go. "I hope you've enjoyed your stay, Vera. It's too short to suit me."

"Me, too. But that's all the time I could steal. I've had a marvelous time, Constance. You and Jerry have made every day a pleasure. He's a very considerate man."

"Yes, isn't he? Sometimes I want to tell him, knock it off, Jerry. Raise your voice, lose your temper, do something that I can resent just for five minutes, will you? But I don't and he doesn't so again I don't. If you follow me."

Vera had to laugh. "Believe it or not, I know what you mean. I've never had my chair held so often in my life and every time I started to light a cigarette—there he was with a match. But don't worry, Constance, I'm sure it will all wear off. It's simply a case of bridegroom nicey-niceness."

Constance, smiling, nodded and dismissed the subject. "About the book, I'll get the rewrites to you as soon as possible. To tell you the truth, I could use the advance. My monthly checks don't go as far as they once did."

"But you've got Jerry to take care of you now."

"His monthly checks don't go as far as they used to either, or so he tells me."

"Well, I'll send the contract as soon as I get back and when you return it I'll mail the check. What with the mail and all, it may take as much as a month, but you know how the powers that be be."

"That will be fine, Vera. Thanks. Ah, good. I can pull right in here and we won't have far to carry your bag. Want me to hail someone to take it for you?"

"No, no, it's not heavy. Goodness, this airport is a busy place. It seems larger to me than when I was last here. Is it?"

"Probably. They're always adding to it. There's a line at your airline check-in, so what else is new? I'll wait for you over here, okay?"

"Listen, you don't have to wait at all, you know. Standing around waiting for a guest to depart must come under the heading of one of the world's most boring activities. So why don't you just leave me and go home."

"If you don't mind, Vera, I just might do that. I'm a little anxious about Jerry."

"About Jerry?"

"Yes, he wasn't feeling too well this morning. That's why he didn't come in to breakfast or say good-bye."

"He sent Alfie in his place with a little note. I thought that was sweet."

"Yes, wasn't it? Well, I will run if you'll forgive me. Here's a kiss for each cheek, the French way. Have a good trip home and hurry back."

"Thanks for everything, Constance. And thank Jerry."

"I will. I'll be in touch soon." And as they turned from each other Constance nearly turned back to say something else—what, she knew not—but didn't because there was nothing else to say.

It was Della, maid to Constance for all her time here, and now maid to Mr. and Mrs. Tosca, who found the papers.

"Miss Constance, what should I do with these?"

"What are they?" Constance was annoyed; she was in the middle of rewriting a chapter.

"I don't know for sure. Papers. They look important. I found them, in this"—she held up a cream-colored plastic bag in her other hand—"in the freezer."

Intrigued, Constance reached for the packet. "In the *freezer?* In a plastic bag?" Sure enough, the papers were cold. She slipped the elastic off one end, opened the top fold, read *The Commonwealth of Anguilla* but no further because Jerry was there, holding out his hand, smiling, saying, "Now don't spoil my little surprise. Give them to me, my dear. You'll know all about it at the proper time."

She handed him the papers and the rubber band, watched him put the pages back together. "I thought I had the perfect hidey-hole"—he beamed at Della—"but I underestimated the cleaning powers of a woman."

"I was just defrosting the freezer, Mr. Jerry. Miss Constance likes me to do that every six months. She says it's easy to keep track of what's in it when I do that. She says she doesn't want any surprises growing in the freezer like ba-pilly—ba-silly . . ."

"Bacilli? Thank you, Della. You'd better get back to your defrosting before everything gets spoiled." Constance waited for the maid to leave. "Have you bought a piece of land in Anguilla?" She was quite put out. Wasting money on land on that sad little island, how could he be so foolish?

"It was to be a surprise. An anniversary gift." He sat in the wicker fan chair. "You aren't pleased? Well, then, I'll give it back, it isn't settled yet, anyway. I only put down a small deposit."

"Which you'll lose, I presume. Where is it, anyway?"

"On the northeast coast. Shoal Bay. A beautiful beach, great spot for a house."

"Shoal Bay. Where Bootsie Baker died. I didn't know you'd ever been there. We didn't go there when we were on Anguilla."

"No. But I'd been there before."

"But when, then, did you buy this anniversary present?"

"When you said you'd marry me. I flew right over the next day to clinch the deal. A hideaway house of our own, I thought that would be fun. Wouldn't it, Constance? Wouldn't that be fun?"

"We can't afford it, Jerry. You know that. Hideaway houses cost money, a great deal of money these days. And we have a perfectly good house right here."

"But it's your house. I wanted us to have our house." With his mouth turned down like that, he looked a bit like Alfie.

"I'm sorry, Jerry." She straightened her chair, ready to return to work. She had discovered that sometimes she had to play the part of stern parent.

"Miss Constance."

Della again. Would they never let her work?

"Yes, Della?"

"We has got us a rat, Miss Constance. I find the droppings behind the freezer and I find in the larder where he eat into a box of cereal . . ."

"All right. I'll mix up some rat poison for you. Have we got any leftovers in the fridge?" Rising, she passed Jerry who still sat in the fan chair. "Run along, Jerry, and send that agreement back, like a good boy. Della, we have some leftover meat loaf, don't we? I'll use that to mix it with, it should make a very tasty last supper for Mr. Rat."

That night, after he'd gone to sleep, Constance searched Jerry's pockets, then his bureau for the envelope he should be sending to Anguilla. She found no evidence at all of the papers. What could he have done with them? He had no other private place other than his bureau, his clothes, and he hadn't been off the property all day. What could he have— Wait. The freezer, having been defrosted, was back in action, purring away in frost-free contentment. Could he have put them back in the same place on the theory that no one would suspect that the papers hav-

ing been found there and removed would be there still?
She slipped out of the bedroom down the hall, into the
kitchen, into the pantry that held the freezer.

Turning on the light, she couldn't help letting out a
small yip. Lying almost at her feet was a large rat, breathing his last. He glared up at her, his small-eyed glance ac-
cusing her.

She stepped around him. She opened the lid of the
casketlike freezer, began to poke and push at the contents
of plastic containers, plastic bags and boxes until she
found it. Yes, she'd read him correctly, he'd replaced the
papers and this time she'd look them over carefully.

Constance turned, frightened by a sound. It was the
rat, twitching violently, his claws scratching at the cement floor. She stepped over him again, holding the skirt
of her nightgown high, and left the larder, shutting the
door behind her.

In a good light, at the kitchen table she reopened the
packet of papers. She had read them all by the time Jerry
appeared at the kitchen door. He held Alfie, a sure sign,
she knew now, that he was setting out to disarm her.

"You found them," said Alfie. "Caught you red-handed.
Snooping."

"It's not an agreement for land on Shoal Bay," she told
Jerry. "These are the papers Horace Albertson has been
moving heaven and earth for. You've had them all the
time."

"Just as I said," Alfie repeated. "Caught. Red-handed.
Lying. We throw ourselves on the mercy of the court,
your honor. Tell him, boss. Tell him how we came by
those papers."

Now Jerry spoke in his own voice. "Bootsie gave them

to us for safekeeping. Horace owed her the money for them, she said. She'd paid with her own money for the leases, the land, the licenses. And she was afraid he might take the papers and never pay her back. Plus, she said, he'd agreed to pay her a bonus. But if he couldn't get his hands on the papers, he'd have to pay up. That's what she said. So she left the papers with me. And I hid them in my freezer. When I came here I hid them in your freezer. People usually don't look inside yellow plastic bags in freezers. Only your maid. I didn't count on a maid who looked inside yellow plastic bags."

"When they found her dead, why didn't you give up the papers?"

Alfie took over. "And be suspected of doing the lady in? We were caught between a rock and a hard place. Bootsie and Jerry and I, we were just friends but would they buy that? We decided we'd just hang on to those papers until the muddy waters came clear."

"You didn't plan to make Horace pay for them? After all, he did owe her money. You said."

"She said. We hadn't ruled it out. After all, why should he get them for free?" Alfie rolled his eyes comically.

"Why, indeed, should he? Why lie to me? Were you afraid I'd come to the conclusion that you and Bootsie were—shall we say in the old-fashioned way—more than friends?"

Jerry replied, "It isn't the sort of thing one tells a bride of two months, is it?"

"Maybe not." She looked down at the papers. "What do we do with them now? Sell them to Horace? Your picking him as best man—did that have anything to do with this? Never mind. What do we do now?"

Jerry and Alfie came further into the kitchen. Jerry set Alfie down in a chair across from Constance. He picked up the papers, once again refolded them and fastened them with the rubber band. "When does Della defrost again?"

"In six months."

"Then—back in the deep freeze. The longer he waits, the more he'll pay. Wouldn't you say?"

She nodded.

He walked to the larder door, put his hand on the knob.

"Jerry."

"Yes?" Without turning around.

"There's a dying rat in there."

"Oh?" He opened the door, switched on the light, looked down. "Correction, my dear. Not dying."

"Oh?"

"Dead."

Constance had not been sleeping well. She tossed and turned so much that she'd moved from her twin bed in the master bedroom into a twin bed in the guest room.

It was the book, she told Jerry.

The rewrite was coming slowly, too slowly to suit her. And one thing led to another in the book, it was like washing the kitchen wall just behind the stove only to find then that the wall by the refrigerator looked terrible. . . . "Just bear with me a little. I'll be all right."

"I wish you'd see Dr. Gibbs."

"I will if this doesn't help. I think one of the problems is that I'm worried about waking you up. If I'm in the guest room I won't worry about that."

"Just as long as you aren't planning on making the move permanent. All those books about rich people with separate bedrooms, I never could understand that. My parents slept all their lives in a double bed."

"They're too hot here. Double beds."

"Yes, I'll buy that. As long as the twins are close together, yes? Tell you what, I'll give you a few days. If you
don't get over this insomnia in a week or so, you'll see the
doctor? Agreed?"

"Yes, agreed. Good night, Jerry. I'm sorry."

"I'll keep him company," Alfie announced.

"Good night, Alfie."

"Good night, Constance." She could have sworn, almost, that both answered at once.

In the guest room she lay awake in the warm darkness,
watching the brilliant stars in the window square of the
night sky.

Susan had determined that she couldn't go on with this.
She was almost certain that Greg killed Pauline Gray to
get those papers. The more she thought of it, the more
positive she was. His behavior of late, just too, too icky
sweet. Sneaky sweet. Like taking her to Anguilla that
time because he knew Horace was over there nosing
around. No, not Horace, Brett! Brett was nosing around. I
was his red herring, you see. If Brett heard anything
about Greg and Bootsie, Jerry could produce me and say,
"But here is my woman." He might even have married
me to keep me from suspecting!

No, no, Greg and Susan had been married for years.
She often plotted, wrote chapters in her head after she'd
gone to bed, but it wasn't working well this night. Come
on, Constance, get back into Susan's mind.

It's getting so that I can't bear to have him touch me
and I can't hide that revulsion much longer. What will he
do when he finds I've learned to loathe him? Do you

think he might decide to murder me? After all, I do know about the papers.

No use. She sat upright in bed.

A star fell in the sky, fell so quickly that she almost missed seeing it.

"Those wills, Roger. I did will my assets to him. Do you know, he's so cheap I'll bet he doesn't have any money at all. You remember how he as much as said he was a rich man when he was talking about no one to leave his money to? Won't he be surprised when he finds I'm not exactly the Barbara Hutton of the literary world. He probably thinks I've made a bundle like Agatha Christie. Wait until he finds out exactly how little there actually is.

"Wait until he finds out? I will not. That would mean I was dead and I don't intend to sit around and let him . . . the only way to be sure is to . . . what did you say, Roger? Why don't I just ask him to leave, then divorce him? Well, for one thing, he might not leave; what would I do then? And for another, French law is not like American law, Roger. I don't know how it's different, I only know it takes a long time to get a French divorce and we signed some sort of a contract. What do I do during this long time? Sit around being afraid of Jerry Tosca?

"Because I *am* afraid of him. Him and his dummy. Sometimes that Alfie seems almost human. Of course he's not. I know he's not. I said it just seems that way. There. You can see the state he's gotten me into. I refuse to sit around and be intimidated by a has-been ventriloquist and his out-of-style dummy."

She got out of bed and went out on the balcony that overlooked the pool. Stars were reflected in it.

"So I think—I think, Roger, that I must do something

positive about the situation. What did Vera say about me? I was getting aggressive? All right, then I must do something aggressive.

"I must kill him. Before he kills me."

She went back inside, got into bed, rolled onto her stomach. "I know just how I'll do it. I'll use Susan's technique. I'll poison him, then put him to drown in the sea. The body may never turn up. But if it does, it will be too far gone for autopsies.

"A picnic lunch, I think. We can go to Friar's Bay, there's never anyone there. I'll make deviled eggs, he loves them and the spices will cover up the taste. And he knows I don't care for them, so I won't have to eat any. Should I eat one so I can say we were both poisoned? No, I won't have to take that risk if it seems that he simply drowned. A heart attack? Yes, that's possible. There wouldn't have had to be any previous medical history, heart attacks can come at any time, and anyway, there won't be an autopsy if the sea does its work. Eggs and fried chicken and a bottle of wine, the condemned man enjoyed his last meal! I'll be certain to put in enough rat poison—he weighs about a hundred and seventy pounds, I think I'd better use two packages. Yes, two. That should do it. Just a tiny bit does for one big rat."

She rolled over on her back. "And I shall be the grieving widow. Oh, yes, and inherit whatever it is he has, he must have some money to be able to live here. I can use it. You left me enough, Roger, but you didn't count on inflation and neither did I and the books are getting harder and harder to write . . .

"Can I play the part of the grieving widow convincingly? Why, of course. You know I've had practice,

Roger, plenty of practice." Oh, yes, there was Constance. Do you know what she is thinking as she stands before her husband's coffin? She is thinking, damn you, Roger Cobble, damn you to hell forever and ever. I loved you, how I loved you and love you still. But you wanted to leave me and we couldn't have that, now could we? Remember how sweetly I said I would think it over? Remember how dignified I was, how sensible? No floods of tears, Roger. No weeping and wailing and gnashing of teeth. Not for you to see.

And finally the decision. Mind made up, like now. Sit quietly in the darkness, holding a gun. Listen hard for footsteps, familiar footsteps. She would know his footsteps anywhere.

Hear the door open. That door always had a tiny squeak. Never could find it, oil didn't help. Quiet footsteps; he didn't want to wake her up.

His shadow was clear—she'd been sitting in the dark, eyes adjusted. She cried out, "Who's there?" and pulled the trigger at the same time. She'd practiced and she was right on target.

Constance, see her there, weeping? Weeping now into her pillow. And after weeping, she fell asleep.

The day was a golden one.

(Of course. What other kind were there? Had she said that before? Golden days? Probably. Strike out *golden*, change it to just plain *beautiful*, don't get too fancy.)

★　　★

It was a beautiful day.

So blue the sky. Once in a while a small powder puff of cloud floated by.

There were no other people there, so they went swimming without suits and then they made love beneath the sea grape vines. They swam again, laughing and splashing. After that, dressed in cover-up shirts, they opened the bottle of Blanc de Blanc and toasted each other.

"Have some deviled eggs, darling." She offered him the covered bowl.

"Wonderful. I love your deviled eggs! And your fried chicken. You make the best fried chicken in the world. What would you like? A breast? A thigh?"

"You know I prefer thighs, darling. The breast is for you. I know you're a breast man."

He laughed boyishly. "You can say that again. How about another egg? I'm starving."

"Salt and pepper?"

"Thank you. I think after we eat I'll stretch out under the sea grape and have a nap. Did you ever see a more gorgeous day?"

"Never."

"Imagine if you were newborn and opened your eyes and saw such a beautiful sky? Wouldn't that be a way to begin life?"

"And suppose you were dying and looked up and saw that? Wouldn't that be the way to go?"

"You read my mind. I was just thinking that very thing. But since we are neither just born or about to die but somewhere in between, let's just enjoy it."

"Oh, I am, I truly am. Have another egg?"

"How about you?"

"You know I don't care for eggs. I think I'm allergic to them."

"All right, here's another chicken thigh. Look, over there! A crab is trying to bury that chicken bone. Look at him dig."

"The bone is bigger than he is."

"Doesn't seem to faze him. More wine?"

"Thanks. That wine cooler works well, doesn't it?"

"Sure does. Gosh, I think I'm getting full. Don't believe I can eat that other breast."

"It will be good for lunch tomorrow. Don't worry."

"Fine with me. I'll just stretch out here. Don't stay too long in the sun, you'll get burned."

"I won't. I think I'll just go down to the sea and rinse my hands, they're all sticky from the . . . Greg!"

"Ummm—"

"Greg. I . . ."

"Susan? Susan? I don't feel so good, I . . . Susan. Come. Help me."

"Greg. I . . ."

"I'm sick. I . . . very . . . sick. What did you do? Susan? Did you? Eggs? The eggs? Of course."

"You bastard. You . . . poisoned . . . the chicken? How?"

"The flour, dear one. Flour for the chicken thighs. 'Cause you skin the breasts and don't flour them. Oh, God, I can't stand up. Oh, God. Don't cry, Susan. I'm sorry. Help me get out of here and we'll forget the whole thing. Help me, Susan."

"Help yourself, Greg, I've run out of . . ."

When all was quiet, a yellow bird (sugar keet) flew out of the grape tree and picked at the leftover food in the picnic basket. He didn't care much for the taste so he flew away without calling in any of his friends.

★　　★

Constance read what she had written, and knew immediately it wouldn't do. She'd come up with this idea that the book might have more impact if they poisoned one another, but it wouldn't do. In the first place, it was awkward. If the flour for the chicken was mixed with poison then all the chicken would be tainted. In the second place, it was god-awful. She put the pages together, ripped them across once, then again.

"I take it you're not happy with this morning's efforts." Jerry appeared in the doorway. "It's noon. How about a Bloody Mary to take the bad taste out of your mouth?"

She dropped the torn pieces in the wastebasket, sighed. "This revision is giving me trouble, I don't know why. Maybe I need a break. Want to go on a picnic? I've made deviled eggs."

"Lovely thought." He handed her a tall glass, filled to the brim with tomato juice and gin and ice. Jerry made the best Bloody Mary she'd ever tasted. "Let's have our picnic here at home. By the pool. Will you join me?"

"I thought we could go to the beach, Friar's Bay, maybe. There's never anyone there. I need to get away from here, I think. I need something different to stimulate me."

"We could take a trip."

"Could we? I guess we could. Where?"

"Another island? Another continent? You name it."

"Can we afford it?"

"Oh, I should think so."

"I don't know about your finances, but I'm anxiously awaiting a check."

"Yes. Your monthly stipend. It will be along. You know the mails here. How about a refill?"

"You made them awfully strong this time, didn't you? It tastes kind of strange."

"I threw in some fennel. Do you think it improves the blend?"

"I guess so. I'm not sure."

"Well, drink it up and give me your considered opinion. Instead of a wine-tasting, a Bloody Mary-tasting, how about that?"

"You haven't finished yours."

"I'm waiting for you to catch up. I've already had two."

"I don't think I like the new flavor as well." She shook her head, handed the empty glass to him. "Make the next one the old way."

"Maybe it needs more Worcestershire." He took the glass inside, was back in minutes. "See if this is better."

She tasted. "It's better, yes, much better. If we did go somewhere, where would we go?"

He sat, legs outstretched, head back. "I don't know. Where would you like to go? South America?"

"How much would that cost? Wouldn't it be expensive?"

He shrugged. "No idea. I'll check with the travel agency if you like."

"I can't help thinking it would cost a lot. Flying down to Rio, for instance, sounds awfully expensive."

Jerry laughed. "Connie, don't be such a miser. It's the Yankee in you, I guess. So we'll each take a little out of our savings socks and fly away. We may not be around forever, you know. What good will all that dough do then?"

She offered her empty glass. "If you feel that way about it, you can pay the fare for everything and then I won't have any pangs of conscience. How about that?"

He rose, bowed, and took her glass. "It will be my pleasure. I'll go tomorrow. Rio, you said, and maybe Peru, and how about the Galapagos Islands?"

Faker. Absolute faker. It was the money he coveted,

she was sure of it now. She remembered the byplay with Barney Gingle. "Tell her the truth, Barney, that I made a mint and threw it away, that I'm not only as poor as Job's turkey, I'm as poor as Job's goat . . ."

How could she have been so foolish, no, more than foolish, downright stupid. Fear, that was what had done it. Fear of age, fear of aloneness, fear of poverty, fear of dying . . .

Well, she'd gotten herself into it. She had to get herself out.

Here he came now. A tray in hand, pitcher of Bloody Marys and two glasses on it. "Let's have a toast," she cried. "A toast to South America—including the Galapagos Islands!"

"Hear, hear." Alfie spoke from his place atop the wicker sofa back. As always, she looked quickly, carefully at him. One day she would catch him with his mouth open when Jerry couldn't possibly be working the controls.

She smiled at the thought and took a long swallow. The smile felt so good that she laughed. She felt giddy, she was getting tipsy. Tipsy, hah! Smashed. The only way to be when you were going to have a poolside picnic complete with deviled eggs and all.

Jerry was saying something.

"What?" She squinted. "You're not drinking. Your glass is still red. That means it's full."

"I said, would you like another drink?"

She blinked once, twice, counted the blinks. The pitcher was less than half full. That made her an optimist. A pessimist would call it half empty. "Yes." No.

"All of a sudden," she said carefully, "I don't feel well. Call Della, please."

"Della's gone home. She finished early because one of her kids is sick. I told her she could go."

"Drink, Jerry. Drink your Bloody Mary."

"But I did drink it, Connie. See? My glass is empty."

She would have said, "But it wasn't a minute ago," but that seemed a lot to say. "I have this awful feeling . . ."

"You don't look too well, Connie, and that's a fact. Tell you what, I'll go into the house and fix you an Alka-Seltzer. Now just lie down like a good girl and I'll be right back. Here's Alfie to watch over you." She saw him, dimly, disappearing, tray and all, into the house.

Alfie, the dummy, suddenly collapsed against her and she tried to push him away but he was too heavy.

She concentrated with all her will. The Bloody Marys, he must have put something (the same, the very same poison for rats?) into the Bloody Marys. She'd underestimated him.

It was funny, it really was. She must tell Roger all about it when the crisis had passed. The thing to do was to vomit, rid herself of the poison. .

She tried again to move Alfie. How could he be so heavy? It distressed her to throw up without a pan, a pail, something. That was funny, too. She was poisoned and yet persisted in being fastidious.

Jerry wouldn't come back, not until it was all over. Well, she'd see that it wasn't all over. She'd show him. It wasn't so easy . . .

"Here you are, Connie. Drink it down. Good old Alka-Seltzer." Jerry, brown eyes warm, held a bubbling glass for her.

"Get Alfie off me."

"Sure thing. Sit up, Alfie. You're out of line. You must have caught a bug, Connie. There's one going around."

She drank thirstily of the salty, medicine-tasting drink. She told herself she was crazy. Jerry wouldn't poison her. Jerry loved her. See, Roger, he even brought me Alka-Seltzer . . . had the Alka-Seltzer tasted funny?

Suppose he wanted to be sure, to really be sure, so he laced the concoction with more of the poison?

He looked down at her, anxiety on his face. What an actor. Oh, what a skilled actor he was. She must get him to leave her so she could rid her system of his venom . . .

"Jerry, leave me—alone. Be all right after a while. Please. Go have lunch. Please, Jerry."

"I don't like to leave you."

"Hate . . . you . . . standing there!"

"All right, all right. I'll go."

Exhausted, she watched him go. Couldn't he move any faster? There. At last. She'd just get up, oh, God, wouldn't her legs hold her? Get to the railing, all right, crawl if you can't walk . . . but what if you couldn't crawl? Force yourself, force yourself. Who said that? Alfie? One day I'll catch you in the act, damn you . . . oh, God, so sick, so very sick. Somebody come, anybody. Agnes, Agnes, where are you now that I need you . . . ?

"Connie?" A call from the kitchen.

She summoned her strength to answer. "Yes?"

"Is it all right to eat these deviled eggs? Or do you want to save them?"

"It's all right, Jerry. Eat . . . all . . . you . . . want."

She thought she'd die laughing.

Voices awakened her. Familiar voices.

"The doctor says she's got this terrific constitution, that's all that saved her." That voice she couldn't mistake. Agnes' voice.

"Somebody or something was watching over her, that's for sure." Vera? Yes, Vera was outside talking to Agnes and she, Constance, was in a hospital and she was alive, she hadn't died after all.

"I almost had a heart attack when I heard about it." A third voice, female voice, good heavens, Elsie's New England tones. Her sister Elsie was outside that door. It must have been touch and go if Elsie had traveled to St. Martin. Elsie hated airplanes.

". . . enough poison to wipe out a village, that's what the gendarmes told me," Agnes was saying.

"How did they happen to show up at just the right time?" Vera wanted to know.

"Well, it was this way." Agnes was at the top of her form, bubbling over with importance. "The gendarmes were still investigating the death of Bootsie Baker. Somebody had told them they'd seen her with Jerry, you see, and they were routinely checking everybody who'd been associated with her, you see? So this very day that it happened was the day they came to call on Jerry. And we know what they found." Agnes' voice dropped theatrically. Oh, the idiot. Shut up, Agnes.

What had they found? Jerry? Jerry dead? If so, what did they think? No matter what, she was in trouble. Go on, Agnes, talk some more. Before I have to face you, I must know . . .

"She was on the gallery and he was in the kitchen. His poison came from the eggs, oh, my, they were loaded with it and he had eaten several. Hers, they figured, came from the Bloody Marys, there was some left in the pitcher, just a little, I understand, but enough to tell . . ."

"I just couldn't believe it when I heard who did it. I mean, Della has been with Constance ever since she came here." Vera sounded doubtful.

"Yes, I know. But Jerry made what amounts to a deathbed accusation. She denies it, of course, and there'll be a trial. But who else could it have been? Both of them full of it, you can't for a minute accuse one or the other and who else was there? You never know what goes on in a person's mind, you know." Agnes, the sage, was speaking. "Someone you think you know very well can have all sorts of evil thoughts about you without you even suspecting."

"Yes, that's certainly so." Elsie sighed. "Do you think she's awake yet? I have to catch my plane at three."

Constance shut her eyes.

"Not yet." Vera spoke from near the door, she'd looked in.

"Who's going to tell her about Jerry?" Agnes wanted to know.

"You're her friend, I thought you were." Elsie clearly wanted no part of it. That must mean that . . . a deathbed accusation? Let us hope . . .

"Good afternoon, ladies." A strange voice, a masculine voice spoke now. "How is the patient in Room Four?"

"She's going to be all right." Agnes sounded pleased. If Agnes weren't such a bore, there'd be a good bit one could say for her.

"Happy to hear it. I'm on my way to visit a sick friend and I hope the news is as good. I wish you a good day, ladies, a good day indeed."

And after he had gone, Elsie asked, "Who was that charming man?"

"He reminds me of a—teddy bear," thought Vera.

"Cad. That's what they call him. His name is Cadwallader, he's been here for ages. Let's peep in again . . ." It was the sound of shuffling, somebody dropping something outside that made her open her eyes.

"Constance!" Vera came through the door with her hands outstretched, followed by Elsie with Agnes bringing up the rear. Agnes wore a sheepish look and carried some dripping hibiscus blossoms.

"I'm sorry," she said, "I dropped the vase."

Constance looked at them; they all wore visitors' expressions of concern. Tell me what I want to know, she begged silently, what about Jerry?

Then, "Connie, my love!" And, "Connie, it's me," and

there they were, the two of them, Jerry and Alfie, beaming, all of them beaming and she could scream.

They moved to both sides of her, all talking at once, all reaching for her hands, and Alfie said, "We were lucky once, ducky. Now we'll make sure never again!" And he winked.